God's Laughter

And Other Heresies

Chuck Meyer

SECOND EDITION

For Dana and Jack
For Debi and Michal

CONTENTS

INTRODUCTION

On January 1, 1980, I arrived at St. David's Hospital to start a Department of Pastoral Care. On January 9, the first memo went out to Department Heads describing what exactly that was: "...based on the Kenny Rogers Pastoral Care Model for Effective Involvement: 'You gotta know when to hold 'em, know when to fold 'em, know when to walk away, know when to run.'" We were a small hospital of 213 beds then (compared with 558 now), and Pastoral Care Memos often contained personal references that everyone would understand, including names of people, hospital incidents, and juicy rumours.

When our Public Relations Director, Jan McCrory, began the monthly hospital newsletter in April of 1980, she asked me to do a monthly column. I called it Pastoral Care Comments, for lack of a better name, and asked for suggestions from staff for another title. Only one employee, Nadine Murphy of Inservice Education, responded with "Clergy Collectables" or "Sanctified Droplets," so I left well enough alone.

I originally compiled the best of those memos and columns into the first edition of this book exclusively for perusal by the St. David's Hospital family. So I was surprised to find that, wherever I spoke around the country, people expressed interest in the stories and commentaries, and found them to be helpful and entertaining regardless of background or familiarity with a hospital setting. Many people encouraged a wider distribution of the material—so here it is, complete with twenty-four new additions including The Last Letter to Nathan.

This is, indeed, the only place where you will find all of the "Nathan Letters." Nathan Brown Joslin is the son of Dana Joslin R.N., and Roger Joslin, who have been my closest friends for the last ten years. Nathan was the first baby to come into my life that I actually liked. It was he who prepared the way for me to consider marrying anyone with a child, which I eventually did, and now he and my daughter Michal are becoming fast friends. It is truly incredible, the turns life takes. Stone Angel Books has begun publishing the Nathan Christmas stories as individual children's books with wonderful illustrations. In the meantime, they can be read aloud to your children only from this collection.

The first edition of *God's Laughter* was dedicated to Dana Joslin and Jack Campbell, whose lives have been intertwined with mine the entire time at St. David's, both professionally and personally. I literally would not have made it through both bad and good times without them both, and I will be forever grateful for their honesty and their willingness to be there again and again and again. They have listened, counseled, laughed and fought with me through all the circumstances of more than a decade, and I look forward to whatever our future together holds.

This second edition adds my wife, Debi, and our daughter Michal to the dedication. They sustain my spirit and maintain my sense of humour through the events of our lives together. And they tolerate the large amount of time allotted to my insatiable penchants for running and writing, providing requested and unrequested suggestions about both.

Our daughter, Michal, is personally responsible for a large number of the stories in this second edition due to her unknowingly pithy sayings, compelling questions, erudite answers, and generally accurate theological view of the universe which usually coincides with (but sometimes challenges) mine. (I am a totally unprejudiced Dad.)

The volume title comes from a story about Michal that most accurately expresses my view of God, and from the fact that you will find the theology expressed here somewhat outside that of mainstream Christian writing. (St. David's Employee Health Nurse Chris Jones says that "outside" is a conservative adjective, but she is now and always will be older than I am and is entitled to be humoured in her erroneous beliefs.)

I started to delete the funeral/memorial sermons that were in the first edition, but decided to leave them in for two reasons. The first is that readers have repeatedly told me how much they enjoyed the stories even though they didn't know the people (which may tell you something about the folks who buy this book.) The second reason is that I like them myself, and I like the richness of feeling and personal warmth they add to the volume.

The funeral/memorial homilies were written for patients that were a part of the old 4 West (oncology unit) family. There were more that could have been added, like the man who had Willie Nelson songs played during his service, or the woman who was buried facing Niemann Marcus with her credit cards in her hand. Hopefully those tales will end up in another volume. For now, enjoy the stories of Jimmy Klutts and Margaret Pfeiffer. The *Letter to Nikky* comes from the memorial for St. David's Director of Social Services, Adele Lorusso.

As with the first edition, the stories follow the rhythm of the Church year. They move from Advent and Christmas through Epiphany and Lent, to Easter and Pentecost and back to Advent again. Thus you can read them in sequential order, or you can pick out titles that sound interesting ("Babies") or relate to your state of mind at the present time ("Hell.")

Special thanks go to Dana Joslin and Dr. Richard Turbin for their proofing of the first edition, and to Julie Hamilton for her excellent editing and painfully accurate suggestions regarding the second one. Thanks are also due to my wife Debi for repeated readings, and discussions at late hours of whether to do this book and what to include; and to Gail Roberts for her helpful comments and feedback. To Doyle Fellers, of the advertising agency of the same name, goes my appreciation for the cover preparation and for his general enthusiasm about the stories.

Where to keep this book seems to be a recurring problem for people. Many readers have told me they keep it by their bedside for night time reading just before going to sleep. This is not particularly complimentary to the author and, therefore, is not recommended. Even worse are the reports of numerous persons keeping the volume in the *bathroom*. One ICU nurse told me that her husband reads it by the hour in there and that she turns my picture over so as not to have me staring at her as she "brushes her teeth." (I am certain this is a euphemism.) I can only assume that the average story is the exact length of the average......bath.

Surprisingly enough, even with ALL THE ADDITIONS AND CHANGES, there are STILL 66 STORIES in the book! (For the Biblically illiterate, that is the *exact number of the books in the Bible*.) This PROVES that the first edition was not just a fluky coincidence but that it is THE WILL OF GOD and that the buying of this book will DEFINITELY increase your personal chances of going to HEAVEN (along with increasing my chances of having a great vacation). In fact, I am SO CONVINCED of this fact that I am offering a *money back guarantee* to anyone who does not get there. Just let me know by registered U.S. Mail and I will happily refund the purchase price—NO QUESTIONS ASKED! (I know the Post Office must exist in the Afterlife, because it always takes an Eternity to get my mail.)

Until that time, enjoy these stories—and keep an ear carefully tuned. The sound you hear in the background—of these stories and of your life—indicates that God isn't finished with us yet, and we most certainly are not yet finished with God; for the sound you hear in the background is God's laughter.

Chuck Meyer
Austin, Texas
May, 1992

BABIES

Babies are obscene. They ingest voraciously, they leak (from both ends) profusely, they shun nice people for no particular reason known to science and goo-goo at others who are known by all to be social outcasts. They drool on perfectly nice clothing, detest expensive toys in favor of pots and pans and spoons, and display their total disregard of modesty at all the socially inappropriate times.

Babies reject and threaten all of our social customs and the alleged stability of our lives. They laugh at the wrong things and are curious at the wrong times. They reject our boundaries and question our assumptions about the importance of things. They know nothing of inflation, crime, pollution, racism, denominationalism, fear of dying, fear of living, designer diapers, nitwits or nuclear war.

Babies draw people together. People swap lies about their babies, in the process of swapping pictures. Babies are a common commodity for us all. We all (with the possible exception of Winston Churchill) used to be one. Babies attract attention and make people smile without doing anything. They naturally evoke touching and cuddling from complete strangers who, if they did that to someone their own age, would be accused of evil living.

Babies evoke hope. They look like everybody. They are universally smart, pretty, handsome, untainted (immediately after changing), successful and all the other things adults wish they were.

Thus it is at this Christmas time of year, in the midst of the annual insanities of political hostages and atrocities somewhere in the world, inflation and recession, the deaths of both the famous and the anonymous, earthquake victims, poverty, church arguments about abortion, overpopulation and celibacy, crass Christmas advertising and commercialism—it is into the midst of this world that "unto us a child is born" who "shall not judge by what his eyes see or by what his ears hear."

The baby Jesus is born into our lives at the wrong place in the wrong time. He confronts our social, political, economic, and religious assumptions. He brings us together. He attracts our attention. He evokes hugging and warmth. He brings hope.

In celebration of His birth, may we join Him in the daring, radical impropriety of loving one another.

HOSPITAL SPANISH

"Glossolalia" is the technical word for "speaking in tongues" (unintelligible language). The early church folks did it and there was a lot of controversy over whether it was good or bad. St. Paul said it was okay as long as there was somebody around to interpret it. That was because he could never make heads nor tails out of what people were babbling about and Paul wanted to know what the heck was going on. Today some people think that if you haven't spoken in tongues you aren't in with God. I am sure that will come as a big surprise to God, who could care less whether I am muttering gibberish or speaking in my usual vulgarities as long as I am communicating for a change.

Anyway, since I once enrolled in a certain course taught at the hospital where I work, I will never have to worry about being *in* with God. The course was entitled "Glossolalia 101"—cleverly disguised as "Spanish for the Hopeless". So as not to be caught teaching such a controversial subject as glossolalia, we never met in the same room twice. Each week you could hear certain people muttering "Donde es the Spanish

Class?" Had we met in the Chapel people would have surely thought it was a Pentecostal Revival Meeting.

The instructor, who was looking for work in North Carolina or Minnesota because his lovely wife was from Brazil and they spoke Portuguese at home, had the patience of Job with us. His task was sort of like explaining nuclear physics to a four year old. Thus the examples of how to remember the number 13: "Comic paper detective—Dick *Trece*'; or the number 5: "What happened to the Titanic? *Cinco*"; or 15: "The screaming coroner on TV—*Quince*". "And what month of the year do you put on your ham and cheese? *Mayo*".

The best part was when we all started speaking in tongues at once. Here is a translation of our class efforts.

"What time is it? It is one burp on Sunday. Does Leenda eat spinach? Yes, the dog is the door. How did you? Fine, thank you very ears. Where are you sick? I am throat cramp in my nose, thank you. Do you ask the cabbage? Yes, my eyes drink the hamburger. Chuck, ask Sherri if she drinks the foot. Yes, Sherri, do you have breakfast at the goat? No, I do not water the room. Marion, does Sherri throw the beer? No, yes, Maria and Sherri swallow the chills. Do you fly the door? Yes, I juice the patient. What day are you rain? October forty coat."

We quickly learned the proper greeting for a new maternity patient: "Como se llama, mama?" Also a common greeting, "Como esta, frijole cabrito?" (How have you bean, kid?) By the end of the course we knew enough to get into a lot of trouble on the units and therefore needed to sign up for "Advanced Glossolalia 102" next semester. What we really needed was St. Paul to interpret our efforts. Oh well, at least we're all in with God.

Buenas fiebre.

LENT

When I was a kid I thought Lent was the past tense of "Loaned." I figured the extra pennies I put in the collection plate were "lent" to the church to pay for all those palms and flowers. As a teenager, I discovered that Lent was that special time of the year when Christians were not supposed to sin. This revelation was especially disconcerting because sinning was one of the few things at which I was really any good. Since many people are still laboring under the same inaccurate information, I hereby provide

A BEGINNER'S GUIDE TO LENT

1. **Lent**—An old Anglo Saxon word (are there any *new* Anglo Saxon words?) simply meaning "Spring", as in "He had a Lent in his step..." The word also means "long days" (as in "Nurses sure put in some Lent in the hospital...")

2. **Shrove Tuesday**—The day before Ash Wednesday. The word comes from "shriving" or confession and absolution by the faithful before the penitential period of Lent. Also called *Fat Tuesday* it is the last chance to use up fats and butter in cooking before fasting in Lent. Episcopalians have Fat Tuesday

Pancake Suppers. These have been copied by Lutherans and Methodists in an attempt to be liturgically ecumenical.

3. **Ash Wednesday**—The first day of Lent. Originally (6th century) ashes were only for people doing penance for awful, notorious, industrial strength sins. Later everybody got into the act so now you can't tell the really awful folks from the half-awful ones, unless they sell the movie rights when the book comes out. The ashes are the remains of last year's palms—an early attempt at recycling and a symbol that worldly power (riding into Jerusalem in public acclaim) is quickly reduced again to dust.

4. **40 Days**—The number of days between Ash Wednesday and Easter Sunday according to the Church Calendar, which is wrong. There are actually 47, but you don't count Sundays because it's a feast day, not a fast day. That doesn't make a bit of sense to me. Everyone knows weekends go much faster than work days. The 40 days were originally a time of intense prayer, severe fasting, and daily teaching for those who wanted to join the church. Today they are an excuse to lose weight, give up coffee, cigarettes or chocolate and make sure everyone knows how righteous we are for doing it.

5. **Palms**—At the prison where I used to work, most people thought Palms referred to a book in the Old Testament. Some of the inmates did too. Their favorite was the 23rd Palm. On Palm Sunday, Palm leaves are distributed to churchgoers in memory of

Jesus' triumphal entry into Jerusalem. (At the prison they were rolled and smoked in celebration.) Episcopalians grow their own species of palm trees which produce leaves in the shape of little crosses. I know because I get one every Palm Sunday.

6. **Maundy Thursday**—This is a toughie to explain to Baptists who think that the only two religious days of the week are Sunday and Wednesday, though they do make an annual exception for Good Friday. The day means "Wash Day" from "maundatum"—"to wash," referring to Jesus washing the disciples' feet at the Last Supper. (John 3.15) A Methodist friend of mine always wondered how you dealt with panty hose in this situation. Fortunately they did not have to worry about that in the 6th century. This night is the last time Holy Communion is consecrated until Sunday.

7. **Good Friday**—Even the Baptists have this one. In typical Christian style we call the absolute worst day of our tradition "GOOD" Friday. It is "good" because Christ Jesus chose to trust God's will instead of his own. The disciples thought it was Awful Friday. They had lost their beloved companion and watched him slowly suffocate on a cross—from a distance of course. They were scared (us next?), angry (why him?), and confused (what next?). And they didn't know yet about Easter. On this day the altar is stripped to symbolize our emptiness and mourning.

8. **Easter Sunday**—More properly called *Resurrection Sunday*. It commemorates the day of Christ Jesus' resurrection and reappearance: also commemorates the day when unnamed thousands are resurrected for their annual reappearance in a church. In Texas it is called *Souther*. Often confused with an anti-church conspiracy called the Easter Bunny who allegedly lays eggs and distributes candy filled with carcinogenic artificial colors and flavors designed to make kids of all ages toothless and hyperactive. Sometimes mistaken for the anesthesiologist who made extra money waiting tables at the local Playboy Club—the Ether Bunny.

Hopefully this Beginner's Guide will enable you to have a meaningful Lent with no sinning. If you find you fail on both counts (meaning and sin), don't worry. There is a place for you in the Episcopal Church with the rest of us.

SHIRT COLOR

An important religious advance in recent years has been the systematic demythologizing of the mysteries of the Holy Order of Ministers. One of the more complex of these holy mysteries and one about which I am often asked is—Clergy Shirt Color.

First some basic guidelines:

1. In answer to those who, with shocked astonishment in their face, comment: "I didn't know you were *allowed* to wear colors."—Neither our bishops nor our mothers tell us what to wear. (Well, most of us anyway.)

2. Although it may be difficult to believe, there is no direct correlation between clergy shirt color and level of holiness. (Indirect correlations are being explored.)

3. Women often get their own shirts/blouses individually made because the clergy shirt catalogues provide selections for women designed by Omar the Tentmaker with tucks in the wrong places.

So there will be no further confusion, I hereby reveal the following clergy shirt color explanations:

Blue—Sky color—Clergy feeling high that day, usually following parish picnic or annual parish meeting at which clergy is retained for yet another term. Lutherans wear this color a lot, neatly offsetting blonde Norwegian hair.

Brown—Clergy feeling earthy, or sinful, or both. May need cheering up, or may prefer to wallow in shirt a while longer. Offer to take to lunch and talk about it.

Yellow—Sun color—Clergy feeling exceptionally brilliant. Do not rain on parade and produce brown shirt. Please humour gracefully and ask for stories.

Green—Clergy feeling growth oriented, or possibly nauseous. Often it is hard to tell the difference. Have note pad and bucket handy for either occurrence.

Orange—Orange always means Halloween or football or the   Great Pumpkin or something fallish. Or it means the shirt was purchased in 1968 and needs to be deposited in the rag bag as psychedelism is now officially out.

Grey—Clergy feeling old and extinguished, I mean distinguished. Frequently used to mask either the appearance of grey hair or Grecian Formula. Make no remarks about aging, refurbishing the church or making repairs to the parsonage. All such comments will be taken personally.

Black—Laundromat Day. Other clergy shirts dirty and possibility of Bishop visiting. Or this shirt also is dirty and clergy knows no one will see the dirt. Please take up donation for new shirt.

For those persons in denominations without official "clergy shirts" the same color schemes apply, except for the last one. If your clergy suddenly appears in a black shirt (with or without a gold chain around the neck) you had better start checking the bank account and be prepared to ante up in the plate. And while you're at it, keep an eye on the choir.

EMPTY TOMBS

Contrary to the usual sentimental mush, the most common feeling associated with Easter is stark terror. Compared with Easter, such limp attempts as *The Shining, The Exorcist* or *The Omen* come off as slapstick comedies.

It would be quite enough to tell the story of a good, decent man who went around helping the very people who praised him with alleluias on Palm Sunday and crucified him five days later. It would even be enough to hear the crucifixion story of nails, a spear in the side, vinegar, slow suffocation and screaming. Either of these accounts would stand the hair of ordinary citizen's head on end. But to top it off we are confronted with the end of the story, the denouement, the most terrifying part of all—the *empty tomb*.

What is so frightening about the empty tomb is its emptiness. We can tolerate loaded tombs, tombs full of caskets, mummies, skeletons, dead folks, live folks pretending to be dead, ashes or remains. What goes against our sense of fairness is to go expecting to find one thing and end up being scared when it's not there. That's probably why all those apostolic pillars of faith who were hiding out in the upper room after the crucifixion didn't believe a word of it when Mary broke in to tell them the Good News.

We too want to discount the event. We would have our tombs full—full of memories, skeletons, guilts, hatreds, bitterness, griefs, unfulfilled loves and hopes, injustices, unrealized expectations of ourselves and others. We are comfortable with our tombs full. We worship our status quo and that of our society in our safe, well arranged storehouse tombs.

But then comes Jesus. And one day we walk to our tomb and find it cleaned out, vacant, spotless—empty. And we are terrified. We know with a certain rush that change is imminent, resurrection is possible and we, like the two Mary's, "run from the tomb in fear and great joy." We are frightened by the new possibilities and overwhelmed by the sense of relief and new life.

Easter is no time for sissies. That's probably why we invented the sweet, colorful, cuddly rabbit and duck indulgences to cushion and insulate us from the real thing. The Easter Bunny is a lot safer than Jesus.

A THANK YOU NOTE TO JIMMY KLUTTS FROM 4 WEST

(Ed. note: Jimmy Klutts died of cancer at age 20 on the 4 West Oncology Unit of St. David's Hospital.)

Dear Jimmy:

We seriously considered beginning this letter with the story about the three legged dog who rode into Dodge City one day, but we thought your mother would never forgive us for telling a joke that ended with the punch line, "Well Mister Dillon, I'm lookin' for the man who shot my paw."

Then we were going to list all of your positive qualities and all we could remember was how much you demanded pizza and hamburgers and Kentucky Fried Chicken instead of all that wonderful hospital food.

We thought about lying and telling everyone what a polite, calm, serene, distant, low key relationship you had with your physician, Dr. John Sandbach, and how you so carefully followed every minute detail of his orders for treatment.

However—being the fine, upstanding, religiously oriented, clean minded, laid back, easy to get along with, unemotional and sober persons that we all are on 4 West—we decided instead to go against the entire tradition of funeral eulogies. We have decided that it would refute our sacred oath to Saint David to be anything less than candid with all of these people who are gathered here in your memory today. We have decided, much to your chagrin, to tell the truth.

And the truth is, quite simply, we liked you. We liked your smile. We liked your sense of humor. We liked the way you always kept your appointments at the Broken Spoke (when we all came to hear your band play and you weren't there). We liked the way you gave flack to Dr. Sandbach and to anyone else who gave it to you. We liked watching you juggle girlfriends and get caught talking to one in the room while another was on the phone. We liked your talent. We liked your music. And although you personally had nothing to do with bringing them into the world, we liked your family. We liked your family partly because they took us in and made us part of them and partly because we did the same thing with them. You raised a good set of parents, Jimmy. We liked you. You were not easy to know, but you were easy to like.

The second part of the truth is a bit more difficult to tell, but to stay true to our code, tell it we must. The second part of the truth is—we are angry. We are angry because you left us. We are angry because we each have some unfinished business with you that will remain unfinished for us for some time. We are angry at your disease and at medicine and at ourselves for our inability to do more and to be more with you. In our more honest moments we are angry even at you for dying and depriving us of your presence—and reminding us of our own deaths that we each must face alone. We are angry at the unfairness of it all, at the short time of your life. And we are angry and scared also at the short time each of us has to be with one another. Your death has made that point poignantly clear, Jimmy, and we are angry and frustrated at being deprived of you and reminded of who we are.

The third part of the truth is easiest to tell, for the truth is—we loved you. Strange as it may seem, that is true of only a few of the many persons with whom we come into contact. But you were one of the few. In fact, there was a uniqueness about you. You were not only easy to like but easy to love. We loved your youthfulness. We loved your words to your songs because they were you. We loved that gaggle of friends and relatives that followed you around day and night worrying over your condition and forgetting about theirs. We loved your loving us.

And so we have come not only to say good bye but also to say "Thank You." Thank you for the time you were with us. Thank you for taking us into your young life and making and keeping us young with you through your words, your actions and your songs. Thank you for not being religious in the traditional sense of the word. Thank you for letting us pray for you and with you and thank you for, in you own way, praying for us. Thank you for putting up with us and for submitting to our ridiculous hospital rituals with patience and impatience at appropriate and inappropriate times. Most of all thank you for being you with all the energy you could muster all the way to the very end.

There is but one more part of the truth to tell, Jimmy. This last part is both hardest and most hopeful; for the truth is we are going on with our lives. A part of us died with you and a part of you lives and goes on with us. For both we are grateful.

Well, that's about it. We are sure that this is the first time that we have been able to have the last word with you.

And so, Jimmy, we send this note to say good bye— and thank you.

"D.T."

It is important from time to time to more closely examine certain outstanding personages of the Bible. This particular Bible Biggie has the unfortunate reputation of being a vile unbeliever, a faithless nerd, and a demanding scoffer. Of course he is none other than "Doubting Thomas", a.k.a. Thomas the Twin (t3), or simply "D.T."

D.T.'s story is well known. He was late for the first Easter and so missed Jesus' appearance in the Upper Room. One cynic said his watch was operating on Texas Time. When he returned, the other disciples told him "We have seen the Lord!" D.T. wondered what specific fermented substances they had been ingesting and why they didn't save any for him, then stated his ill-fated, dastardly line: "Unless *I* see the scars and put *my* hand in his side *I* will not believe." Boo. Hiss. Boo.

Then (a week later) D.T. managed to make the meeting. Jesus appeared again and went straight to him telling him to touch the nail scars and put a hand in his wounded side. D.T. then (of course) responded "My Lord and my God." It is assumed that meant he now believed. I would if it had happened to me. And that, indeed, is the point.

D.T has been badmouthed by pious Christians for centuries for his alleged unbelief. As usual, he has been quoted out of context. The truth is that he was asking no more for himself than the others had received. If we look at the paragraph before his story (Jn. 20.19) we see that it was not until the *other* disciples saw Jesus' hands and side that *they* believed it was the Lord. When Jesus first walked in and talked to them they ignored him. It was only *after* the viewing (and probably touching) of his wounds that they recognized him and believed.

In this light, D.T.'s request is reasonable and equitable. The amazing thing is that Jesus took him seriously enough to reappear and go straight to him and answer his request. The point is not the stubborn unbelief of a faithless disciple at all but rather the incredible good news that Jesus takes the initiative to answer us so that we *will* believe the obvious facts about who he is and who we are. Jesus is not interested in playing testing games. He is up front with us when we ask him to be.

That is the point. D.T. cared enough to be demanding of God. He showed us that if we're serious about this business of faith it is important to ask too much rather than too little. Most of the time we chicken out on God and don't ask enough. We protect God from what we consider to be failure with our lightweight requests.

D.T. is one of the few shining examples of Biblical belief, contrary to popular opinion. So the next time you find yourself shaking in your boots and being labeled a faithless nonbeliever, just remember that you are in good company with the rest of us doubting, demanding Christians who have an existential case of the D.T.'s.

PRISONERS OF HOPE

Zechariah never did get a lot of press. He is not usually the first person that comes to mind when people hear the word "prophet." He is hardly ever mentioned at cocktail parties and has never been on the cover of People Magazine. Even in theological circles he is known as one of the "Minor Prophets," and is lumped together with the likes of Micah and Ezra. "Minor" refers to the fact that his book is smaller than the "major" dudes like Jeremiah and Ezekiel and is not a reference to his ministering to those who dig for coal, or a reflection of his not being able to buy beer.

As is frequently the case in such matters, this "minor" prophet had a giant impact on the believing community. His major (so to speak) contribution, in addition to coining the phrase "The Satan" and furthering the cause of angelology, was to refer to the people of God as "prisoners of hope."

Interesting phrase, that.

To be a prisoner of hope would be to live in eager expectation, refusing to bow to the idols of despair and greed, ignoring the faddish demands of societal peers to conform, condone and consume, denying that more is better, might is right and possessions are power. To live as a prisoner of hope is to be at odds with the values of our society. But because we are unwilling to pay the price for that position we live as prisoners of other things and pretend that we can be God's people at the same time.

Instead, we are prisoners of success, or progress, prisoners of popularity, prisoners of piety or sloppy sentimental religion, prisoners of vengeance or bitterness, prisoners of rescuing or demanding, prisoners of disease, prisoners of personal comfort. And our lifestyles and personal interactions are determined by these prisons we choose for ourselves.

Now it is easy to confuse optimism with hope, though they are not the same. The Bible is not optimistic about people - it is hopeful. Optimism is in fact a kind of wishfulness that frequently results in despair and desolation. Optimism usually requires that a patient recover completely; to be hopeful implies that whether the person lives or dies, he or she is okay, forgiven, loved, safe, comforted, accepted.

Zechariah, true to his prophetic role, holds up a mirror in front of us and asks us to examine the prison we have chosen. He asks that we abandon our current cells of security, piety, nationalism, power or optimism and choose to use our courage to become, with him, prisoners of hope.

TRANSFIGURATION

On August 6, the church celebrates the Feast of the Transfiguration (Mat.17). Jesus took Peter, James and John up on a mountain and was transfigured before them. In a blinding flash of light, Jesus was revealed as the Christ—and the world was so radically changed as to never be the same again. In this light our inner darkness is shattered, we stand revealed as the people we are, and we clearly see the freedom and possibilities before us.

In the reflected light of Christ Jesus' presence we have new insight into history, nature, society, culture, personality. His light is all pervading, all encompassing, revealing parts of ourselves we would prefer to keep hidden, affirming our strengths, healing our weaknesses.

In this explosion of light we too are transfigured. We are called to follow another reality than that which is seen by the world. And we can never go back. Once transfigured, we no longer have the luxury of living in darkness, in blindness to people's needs, to the hungry, to the naked, to the sick, to the imprisoned, to the lonely. The transfiguration is permanent.

On August 6, 1945, the first atomic bomb was dropped over Hiroshima. In a blinding flash of light the world was so radically changed as to never be the same again. In that single instant our lives too were transformed unalterably, as that light has spread its toxic message from country to country. That cancerous light is all pervading, all encompassing, revealing parts of ourselves that we would like to keep hidden—our will to power, our domination, our selfishness. This nuclear light is all demanding, requiring our attention, our worship, our resources.

And so we are confronted with two clear choices. We can see ourselves in the blinding light of Christ Jesus, the light of healing, the light of transformation, the light of hope. Or we can see ourselves basking in the worldly light of nuclear holocaust, the light of pretentious power, the light of inane domination, the light of eternal darkness. We make that choice daily in the things we do or do not do, the things we say or do not say.

It is ironic that the newest nuclear submarine that has the capability of ending our world in a final fiery transfiguration has been named Corpus Christi—the Body of Christ.

MARRIAGE FEAST

The parable of the marriage feast (Mt. 22.1-14) was
The Original Raw Deal. As you recall, the story is about
a king who invites people to a marriage feast but nobody will come. In fact, the second time he sends his
servants out with embossed invitations, the servants
are all killed. The king then retaliates, kills the original
invitees and, after everything is tidied up a bit, sends
other servants out to invite anybody off the streets—
both good and bad. When the wedding hall is filled
with such street people, the king wanders in and spots
one guy sitting in a corner trying to balance a paper
plate on one knee and his wine cup on the other, and
the king notices right away that the guy is "without a
wedding garment." With the disdainful flick of an eye-
brow, the king signals to his bouncer to throw the
bum out of the castle into the "outer darkness where
people weep and gnash their teeth."

And this, Jesus tells us, is what the Kingdom of
Heaven is like. Well, hooray. Something to look forward to, huh?

At least at first blush, there seem to be some difficulties here. Compare this description, for instance, with all that pearly gate, angel harps and streets of gold stuff. According to Jesus, the Kingdom of Heaven (K of H) started out as a good idea but before they got to the guacamole dip it resulted in excuses, rejections, murder one, civil warfare, and a perfectly innocent guy getting the gong because he didn't rent a tux. The K of H, then, unlike the usual descriptions we hear about, is a pretty normal place, just like the rest of the world we live in, the institutions and companies where we work, and even our places of worship.

Secondly, the K of H includes "both good and bad." What a shock to the Perfectly Pious who think they're the only ones with reserved seats. I am reminded of a poem recited to me by a lovely little white haired woman by the name of Mrs. Margaret Kreisle:

"I dreamed death came the other night and heaven's gate swung wide. With grace a kindly angel ushered me inside. And there to my amazement stood folks I'd known before. Some I had judged and labeled unfit for heaven's door. Indignant words sprang from my lips, but never were set free. For every face showed stunned surprise. Not one expected me!"

Finally, the guy getting bounced indicates that the K of H involves demands and responsibilities. We are all invited in to the festivities, both the good and bad parts of ourselves and our society. But the church is more than a preppy social club. Our symbol is the cross, not the alligator, or designer label. There is some preparation required on our part (the "proper wedding garment".) It is not enough to simply present our bodies and expect to be welcomed.

Preparation involves honesty with one another; it means a commitment to our brothers and sisters who are poor, outcast, lonely, infirm and who are economically, politically or socially powerless. To be "clothed" involves a personal awareness of one's abilities and weaknesses and a sense of fairness in dealing with others who are, after all, just like us. Lastly, it is to accept total responsibility for choosing the marriage feast or the gong.

JESUS LETTER

(This letter was left on my desk with a note on the front to "Please Forward".)

Dear Jesus:

Howdy. Everybody else writes letters to the fat guy with the white beard and natty red suit so I thought I'd write one to you. I personally don't see how anyone with such lousy (cardiac prone) eating habits and such bad taste in tailors can laugh all the time, do you? I'm glad you dress in earth tones and eat fish.

Well, how are you? Fine I hope. Are you getting ready for your birthday party? We are. Has it really been another year? Where *does* the time go? Seems like every time I go to church they're either singing Christmas carols or handing out Palm branches. Wonder why that is?

I was thinking the other day about why we give gifts to *each other* on *your* birthday. If people did that on MY birthday, I'd be upset, aren't you? What good is a birthday if you don't get lots of loot that shows people love, respect and cherish you dearly? Then I decided I know why—it is because you and I give each other gifts all year long, right? You give us abundance of life and we give you scarcity and hoarding. You give us a fragile earth full of natural resources and we give you pollution and litter. You give us open arms of welcome, we give you no room at the inns of our lives. You give us unbounded intellect, we give you destructive weapons. You give us the power of love, we give you love of power. You give us unconditional forgiveness, we give you blame for our misfortune. You give us an occasion of beauty, gentleness and rebirth of humanity, we give you commercialism, obligations and Santa Claus.

No wonder December is the most depressing time of the year. Your birthday recalls to us who we have been and what we have and have not done. Perhaps we spend this season trying to do for and give to *each other* to balance out the junk we have given to *you* all year.

But this year it's different, Jesus. I'm giving YOU a gift. It is something you've never had before. It's not a processor or a microwave either. It's not a cute puppy or a useless gift that you'll throw out before January 1. I don't know what you'll do with it, but I would like you to take care of it, nurture it, keep it fit, watered and in good shape so it will last a long, long time. I hope you don't get tired of it or want to pitch it out when it doesn't perform well. I want you to watch over it and make sure it wears out rather than rusts out. Don't use it all the time, though, and be sure to give it time to rest and get its shape back. I sure hope you like it. It's all I've got—I'm giving you *me*.

Happy Birthday, Jesus. Write back soon.

Billy Bob

A LETTER TO NATHAN

(Nathan Brown Joslin is a 7-month-old friend of mine.)

Dear Nathan:

How in the world will I ever explain Christmas to you? It is important to me to do so since this is your first time at it and I don't want it to catch you with your diaper down, so to speak.

Nothing personal, Nathan, but I do not even like babies. When it comes to kids and dogs, I have a reputation for being a little to the right of W.C. Fields. I have never understood why parents think that their homely little bundle of squalling wrinkled flesh with a few strands of hair and an aroma that would knock out an elephant is cute. I have always greeted close baby encounters with horror, never knowing what the tiny creature will do next and which orifice it will choose to do it from.

Then you came along. You came into this world not caring where you were or at what hour you inconvenienced everyone. You barged right into our lives, into my life, when I was not ready, Nathan, crying, demanding, disrupting, separating, joining together in new ways. And you all the time unaware of who you were, what you meant, simply going along being yourself.

I have been so proud to be your Uncle Chuck. But do you care? Certainly not. You greet everyone the same and play no favorites. If I come to your house to play with you you cry and crawl away. If I come to visit your Mommy and Daddy you crawl up in my lap and drop toys for me to pick up so you can drop them again and gurgle. You are so unpredictable, Nathan. The only thing certain about you is uncertainty.

And you have no sense of timing or diplomacy or courtesy at all. Right in the middle of holding and hugging, you spit up all over the polo horse on my shirt. I bounce you on my knee and you do unmentionable things with impossible stains on my designer jeans. I bring you fancy presents from impressive stores and, ignoring the toy, you play with the paper and ribbon. I put my finger in your tiny hand to play with and you put it in you mouth to chew on, drooling down my wrist and making the monogram on my cuffs soggy. It's like you live in a different world, as though you march, or rather crawl, to a different drummer, Nathan.

What is it, then, that I like about you, that keeps me coming back for more? Is it because of what appears to be your innocence? You know nothing about wars and nuclear holocaust, about territories, boundaries or property. If it's there you think it's yours to play with. Is it really your innocence, or that you know something that we, that I, have forgotten, denied or ignored?

Or do I like you because you pay no attention to all of the social customs I work so hard to constrain myself within? Perhaps I envy your freedom, Nathan. If I walk away from someone they blame me for their hurt. If I spit up on their polo horse they get angry. If I play with the paper and ignore the gift they call me insensitive. I wish I could hear the drummer you crawl to once again.

I think most of all I like you because you're funny. You are like the circus clown who points to the supposed seriousness of life in the three rings and doubles over in laughter. You're funny because you're so inappropriate and you make me laugh at my, and the world's, silly and sometimes insane appropriateness.

But here I am rambling when I was supposed to be telling you about Jesus, this baby in a stable who bursts into our lives at the wrong times, makes inordinate statements, fills us with love for Him, for one another and for ourselves, disregards our social customs, crawls to a different drummer and even by his inappropriateness in our world is an occasion for our anger, our laughter, and our hope.

Well, I can see that it will not be necessary to explain Christmas to you now because, my dear Little Nathan, you have just explained it to me.

Love,
Uncle Chuck

EPIPHANY

Now that we have survived the Christmas Holy Days, we can joyfully enter the next season of the church year, Epiphany. This season is symbolized by the three wise men or "Magi" who followed the star and found Jesus in the stable, delivering to him their gifts of gold, frankincense and myrrh. Some orthodox churches celebrate Christmas Day on January 6 (Epiphany) and give gifts then. This makes lots of sense. You not only avoid the Christmas rush, but you can get everything on sale.

The word "epiphanos" means "to show" or "to be revealed." In this season we celebrate the "showing" or "revealing" of Christ Jesus to the whole world. Traditionally, this has been done through the Magi. In one story they represent youth, middle and old age. In another they are of three racial backgrounds. In any case their meaning is clear; the gift of God to us is universal and not exclusive. The gift is to all and not just to some.

This is not a very popular way of thinking today and probably wasn't back then either. We like to think *exc*lusively rather than *inc*lusively. Our school is better than their school; our company is better than their company; our nation is better than their nation; our religion has the truth and their's doesn't; our morals are better than their morals. The Bengals are better than the Forty-Niners.

While exclusive and restrictive thinking might be interesting and sometimes fun (as in football), it is definitely not what's happening in the Kingdom of God. If we take God's message to the shepherds and the wise men seriously, then we can never be restrictive or exclusive. The Kingdom of God contains no distinctions between Greek or Jew, male or female, lawyer or waitress, roughneck or surgeon, rich or poor, Baptist or Episcopalian, short or tall, pretty or ugly, American or Russian.

The message of Epiphany is tough to hear. We want God to be OUR God OUR way, sort of like Burger King. No wonder the leaders of the earth were trying to bribe the Magi to find out where Jesus was so they could kill him. This free, inclusive, non-restrictive, universal Jesus posed, and still poses, a threat to national security. An inclusive nation is a nation with no need of defenses. An inclusive world is a world at peace.

The tiny baby in the stable presented the simple message of "love one another." The Magi of Epiphany, whoever they were, represent the beginning of that message of inclusiveness and the universalism of God's caring for the whole world, indeed the entire universe. It must be tough to be God; who would you root for in the Super Bowl?

FEAR

Fear is an interesting emotion. It is probably the motivating force behind most of our decisions. One could argue that fear and love are flip sides of the same coin.

There are many fears—fear of failure, fear of being disliked, fear of rejection, fear of aging, fear of people knowing us as we really are, fear of death, fear of God, fear of Mike Wallace showing up at your door to interview you.

Some people live bouncing from one fear to another, like a steel ball in a pinball machine, assuming that the longer they can keep bouncing, the more points they score in the game of life. Others never put the quarter in the slot and so hope to avoid all fears by never coming out of the chute. They huddle with the other passive pinballs, believing that there is safety in lonely inactivity.

Jesus' story about the talents (Mt. 25.14-29) is instructive here. The master in the parable gives one servant five talents, another two and another one—then leaves town. Later he returns "to settle accounts." The first and second persons have doubled their talents and therefore find favor. The third has hidden his in the ground out of fear of the master and so returns the same as he received, for which he is rewarded with the old "outer darkness" routine.

The truth is that fear is irrelevant. There is and always will be something to fear. A life lived in fear results in spending eternity (present and future) in the "outer darkness." Jesus calls us instead to a life of risk. We are to go out and risk our talents, not merely bouncing off obstacles like pinballs but rather encountering and encompassing those obstacles, facing fears and engulfing them, even demanding growth and gifts from the very things we fear. We are to take what we've been given and use it, risking it in the world around us with people and institutions.

The outcome is shown in the parable. To risk is to strengthen and grow. To bury the talent is to die. But the parable is not a bulwark for capitalism, as it is frequently seen. The people with the talents do not congratulate themselves on amassing a well-deserved fortune. Nor do they use it as power over those who have amassed less. Rather, the results of the risking are returned to the master in the story, since they were his to begin with and were only loaned to us.

As we move through the Lenten Season of introspection may we, instead of hoarding or burying our talents, choose to risk them. May we also return the results of that risk to the One from whom our talents came. May we offer thanks to God for the chance to have those talents here for a while. And when Mike Wallace appears at your door with a camera, invite him in for coffee and ask *him* questions.

A LETTER OF INTRODUCTION FOR MARGARET PFEIFFER FROM 4 WEST

(Margaret Pfeiffer died on the cancer unit. She would haunt me if I revealed her age.)

Dear God:

We do not do this for everybody. In fact, the person for whom this letter of introduction is written is the first person for whom we have done this. We write the letter out of our deep love for both you and her, and also out of our sincere concern for you both. We on the 4 West Oncology Unit at St. David's Community Hospital have known Margaret Pfeiffer for nearly two years. Since we were totally unprepared for her entrance into our lives, we thought you might want some background information so you could be prepared for what she will do to yours.

First of all you should know that Margaret admired elegance and intelligence. Like one of her heroes, Miss Jean Brodie, Margaret always appreciated the creme de la creme from her pink pianos to her Gibson Girl pictures. If you have need of a millinery shop, Margaret

Pfeiffer will be the one you'll want to run it. She will call it Le Margret and will stock only the finest halos and gowns. Please do not ask her about a certain French parasol she left behind as it would be an indelicate question for such a lady of breeding. We are not sure how such an admirer of finery managed to put up with the likes of the 4 West crew but she seemed not to notice our plebeian ways and appeared delighted to hold court with us in her room at a moment's notice.

You should be aware that Margaret was an avid reader of books, especially biographies. She knows who begat who in every royal family in history. While most people's closets are stocked with food, dishes and kitchenware, Margaret's were packed to overflowing with books. She still has some on order and you will have a difficult time convincing her not to come back to pick them up. The saleswoman at the bookstore knows her well. Once when Margaret was inquiring about a certain book, the woman told her not to buy the hardback because the book would be out in paperback in only a few months. Margaret responded in her typical style with "Girl, I can't wait that long. I'm dying of cancer." Margaret was not known for her subtlety.

She was also able to get away with things nobody else could. Who else would slip on a red garter she'd gotten at a pizza parlor and wear it down to x-ray? And she had so much fun with that, that she wore it to surprise Dr. Sandbach when he came in to examine her. We understand that all the Darter sisters are like this and so, as you probably know by now, you are in for some fun and some trouble with Billie, Maud Ann and Margaret plotting and planning together.

You should also know about Margaret's penchant for castles and croissants. She had her own castle in her house and she knew every nook and cranny of the ones built by King Ludwig in Germany, even though she'd never been there. We would like to recommend you send her for a visit. Also please tell her that the poster of the castle now proudly hangs on the nursing station door so we think of her daily in our comings and goings. We also think of her as we pass the Texas French Bread Bakery on Guadalupe, where Margaret bought (or had bought for her by Darrell, her Hospice volunteer) her favorite croissants and French bread. Do not, however, make the mistake of assuming that just because Margaret knew about German castles she also liked German beer. Two of us conspired to "kidnap" her from her hospital room and spirited her off to Sholz's one rainy night to quaff a cold one, only to find that Margaret didn't drink. She did, however humour us by having "two HUGE Dr. Pepper's darlin.'"

Quiet as it's kept, Margaret also had her soft side. She didn't talk about it very much, but it was obvious to anyone who knew her well. Her patience with teaching mentally handicapped children was born out of her care and love for those less fortunate than she. Her love for the other patients, especially Frankie, Francis and Cleva was shown in her many visits to them and the weekly 4 West Support Group. As embarrassed as she would be to hear it, it is clear that your love was at work in her. You might tell her that if you get a chance.

Margaret's love was also evident for Bill and Rowena and for her family. Though it was often an independent, even a distant kind of loving, it was nurturing in its own way. To say that Margaret Pfeiffer was fiercely independent is an understatement. Be prepared for a lady who will not let anyone do anything for her—at least at first. We are gratefully aware that Margaret's gift to us was to let us get close to her, to know her, to do for her, and to love her. And it is an eternal gift to us that she, in her own gracious, funny and elegant way, loved us right back.

It occurs to us that this letter may in fact be too late. Margaret may have already captured your heart as we let her capture ours. She is great fun, God. We want you to keep her and those with her well and as much out of trouble as possible. Answer as many of her innumerable questions about religion and Jesus and the church as you are able. Be as patient with her as she was with us.

We will never forget her. She was truly a gift to us for this short period in which our lives were intertwined with hers. She reminded us of our faults, of our foibles, and of the fun that we can have when we "become as little children."

Tell her again that we loved her. And, if possible, please arrange to have her on our welcoming committee. Tell her good-bye for us. We know she will bring you as much joy and love as she brought us. If you have any further questions about this very unusual, very wonderful, very lovely lady, you know where we can be found.

Sincerely,
The 4 West Crew

CONSTRUCTION

I knew I was in trouble when they put the big piece of plywood over my window. My office suddenly took on the appearance of a well-furnished coffin. Even now as I write, the walls are reverberating with the sounds of bricks being smashed and cement being drilled into. I prefer the smashing. It is over momentarily. The drilling sounds like the upper floors are being strafed by the Luftwaffe.

In the midst of a communion service the other day, as the Hospital Chapel became a reverberating blur and my voice rose to the 180 decibel level to counter the upstairs strafing, I decided that all this noise was actually a good thing.

It is, first of all, a reminder that the church exists in the world. Contrary to the separationists, the church is not a secure place to hide out until the Second Coming. The church is to be relevant to the daily lives of people, affecting everything they do as it is also affected by world events. Theologian Karl Barth argued that the Gospel should be preached with a Bible in one hand and a newspaper in the other.

The omnipresent noise is also a reminder of the Holy Spirit. It is everywhere! It is always with us, from the parking garage to our work areas to lunch to meeting rooms. It is especially in places where we don't want it, like restrooms and lounges. Also like the Holy Spirit, it is a constant disruption, reminding us that the only thing constant in life is change.

Another redeeming aspect of the construction noise is its lesson about pain. There is an interesting belief preferred by many people that life should be free of pain. This belief is partly responsible for our drug-oriented culture. Coffee, aspirin, valium, sugar, diet pills and tranquilizers all attest to the belief that pain is an unnecessary intruder into an otherwise euphoric existence. The blessed noise around here, however, witnesses to the fact that life is not a choice of pain or no pain. Rather we choose the pain of growth involving giving up old images and cherished, comfortable ways of life; or we can choose the pain of staying as we are, continuing old patterns that no longer serve us well and digging ruts into graves. We can choose the pain of change or the pain of maintaining the status quo.

Finally, the construction is a reminder of the reality of hope. The noise will end (as will *all* our noise one day), the new areas will create joy in our hearts, and the plywood will be removed from my window. Maybe that is what the early church meant by "resurrection."

THE FOURTH COMMANDMENT

A friend once told me that when he was a kid there were two seasons of the year—school and summer. It occurs to me now, as an alleged grown-up, that there are still two seasons of the year—work and vacation.

Strange as it may seem, many people detest vacation. Leisure time, time off and vacation time are seen as obstacles to overcome. It is not that these folks love their work; rather they seem never to have learned to do anything else, like play, rest, observe or listen.

Other people *know* what to do with time off; they just feel guilty about doing it. Leisure time for them is inconsistent with the Protestant Work Ethic. (Does this mean Roman Catholics are unaffected by this disorder?) The highest value is work, hard work preferably, hopefully with some miserableness or suffering attached. There is not only an incredible amount of narcissism underlying this attitude, but also a rather common misreading of the Bible, as we will see.

A third group of folks are those who not only *take* vacation and time off—they *live* for it. For them the only reasonable goal of work is to make enough money and accumulate enough time off to play. Work is a means to an end, a minor inconvenience to obtain the highest value—time off.

The Biblical perspective on vacations is found in Exodus 20.8 and Deuteronomy 5.12; both versions of the Ten Commandments. Here God commands that people will "Remember the Sabbath day." Sabbath, by the way, is not just Sunday. The Hebrew word means "rest."

God knows our desires for power, popularity, and wealth, our tendency to want to accumulate, demand and control. And so God builds in for us a breather. God *commands* us to take a break, get some distance, knock it off, be quiet, go play. Work is to be *balanced* with time pursuing other interests or perhaps pursuing nothing.

The function of the Sabbath that we are commanded, not politely requested, to take, is to get our lives back into perspective, to re-learn who is really in charge of the universe, and to renew our relationships with God and each other. And all of this (sorry, Protestants) without the slightest hint of guilt. To observe the Sabbath commandment is, in fact, to know the real meaning of recreation (re-creation); it is to allow ourselves time to be recreated in *God's* image instead of the one we have constructed for ourselves.

One of the comments I hear from dying or seriously ill patients and their families is the wish that they had taken more time off together: traveling, looking, experiencing, re-creating with each other. Many people put off vacations all their lives, only to find no time left. So the next time someone chides you for taking time off, just tell them that you're aware life is short— and that you're keeping Commandment Number 4.

CURRENT EVENTS

Reading the Insight Section of the Sunday paper is part of my weekly ritual exercise in futility. Week before last, all on one page, were horrifying statistics on Hiroshima, a proposal for the irrevocable opening of Western and offshore lands to commercial exploitation, and a story outlining how current economic policies will result in disaster. It made Job look like he got off lucky.

There are three religious responses to this sense of helplessness in the fact of what, in high school social studies, we used to call "current events." The first is the "God is Dead" approach. These folks think God (or the Force) created everything and then split, leaving us to sink or swim entirely on our own. Everything, therefore, from pollution to intraocular lens implants is up to us alone. Their motto might be "We Try Harder." Relying totally on human intellect and human creativity, they believe all our problems can be solved by us. Unfortunately, this group has not yet come to terms with human nature and its insatiable will to power.

The second religious response is the "God is Boss" groupies. These folks smile a lot because they believe that everything that happens is God's will, from nuclear holocaust to stillborn infants. Since God is in charge, they argue, there is nothing to be done. All is in divine order. God will fix it in the end. Trees and mountains and water and atomic particles are all in God's control. All that matters is personal salvation. Stand back and let God run the show. The Insight Section is a catalogue of the latest wonders wrought by God. Obviously, none of these folks live in Beirut.

The third response is based on Paul (Apostle, not McCartney). He called us "co-creators with God." Believing that God is still active in history and that we humans are to use our talents, time and power to influence "current events," these folks might be called the "God Is With Us" bunch. Praying with their feet, hands, votes and bank accounts, they have the Biblical audacity to see themselves as equal partners with God, co-creating His kingdom here and now. For them the Insight Section is a feedback source, or a report card. It spurs them on to more activity while still recognizing part of the work will be and is being done by God.

There are of course medical, economic and political ramifications to each of these religious positions. For me, the third is the most realistic Biblically based response to history: "His story" in which we have a part.

COME TOGETHER, OVER ME

Jesus took a long time to die.

The Romans had crucifixion down to a science. They could increase or decrease the time and pain of the death by varying how far apart or close together they nailed the arms onto the cross beam, how far up or down they placed the foot pedestal, and whether or not they broke the person's legs to prevent pushing themselves up to relieve breathing. Sometimes drugs were given (by sponge to the mouth) either to alleviate the suffering, or to revive people so they could be more lucid during their death.

It was death by suffocation. As the muscles in the arms and legs weakened, the body sagged and the diaphragm thrust up into the chest, choking and cutting off breath.

Three hours was a long time to die. But in that three hours something happened to change the lives of the people gathered around Jesus. Something happened to galvanize a rag tag group of disbelieving, abandoning, frightened individuals into a force that would change forever the history of the world. Something happened to turn abject denial and painful death into an affirmation that would survive persecution, martyrdom and even popular commercialization.

It was as though the diminishing of Jesus' life on the cross was paralleled by the empowerment of the disciples' lives in their various hiding places in Jerusalem. His final cry of death was the birth cry of those who had followed and forsaken him, who now were filled with new power to be him in the world to one another.

"Come together, right now, over me."

The patient took a long time to die.

His disease was insidious, unstoppable. For three weeks we watched as he became incontinent of bowel and bladder, his eyes grew dim and sunk into the black pits of sockets, he grew weaker and unable to ingest food or water, finally becoming demented, his face seizing in a grimacing death mask.

Three weeks was a long time to die. But in those weeks many who had abandoned him earlier returned to visit, and those who were furious or terrified of his death were comforted. The varied array of people walking in and out of his room—friends, loved ones, brothers and sisters, parents, caregivers—all had to talk with each other, eat snacks and drink coffee with each other, lean against walls and sit on couches together. And they all had the same focus—him.

By the time he died the people around him were bonded. His last, bird-like gasp of air was paralleled by a hurricane spirit rush into their souls. His death was their birth as a new creation that had not existed before in their previous anger, pride, frustration, condemnation, fear and judgement. They were transformed and they would carry his death and this moment together for the rest of their lives. They would tell and re-tell the story and, sometimes, the hearer would nod and know and join the widening circle.

"Come together, right now, over me."

Jesus' death was empowering to the disciples. This patient's death, and the similar deaths of so many others, pulls together and empowers those in his or her entourage, no matter how disparate or antagonistic. Perhaps that is what is most frightening to us about death. Perhaps it is not the finality of death, or the unfairness of it, or the horrendous loss and absence that we fear. Rather it may be the possibility of empowerment, of change, of coming together with those we dislike or distrust by means of the great equalizer—death.

It is that bonding that Jews and Christians re-enact in their seder and shabbat and communion services (to "become one"). It is that same communion that we re-enact each day we come together with our families and our co-workers and our friends, when we gather, perform our rituals together and leave together bonded more indelibly to each other.

"Come together, right now, over me."

And we do. Thanks be to God, we do.

GETTING HIGH

(Vacation journal notes)

Well, I guess it is time to come out of the closet about this—I like being high. The higher the better. It is exciting. It is fascinating. One can picture things that one could not picture before. Life and surroundings have a completely different perspective.

No, I am not talking about drugs, alcohol, or chemical substances. I am talking about physical elevation, altitude, height. Looking out from a mountain top, from the bell tower of a cathedral, an observation platform reached by ski gondola or funicular—all are experiences that are breathtaking and mind expanding. And the higher the better.

So here I sit, overlooking the quaint city of Heidelberg. I have spent the last two hours climbing a series of mountain trails. I am out of breath, thirsty, and sitting on a bench looking down onto a blanket of *fog* that completely obscures anything from visibility.

This is not the first time this has happened. I have spent more hours than this climbing to the top of various mountains on foot, driving to the top of a volcano, trekking up church steeples, taking elevators and other mechanical inventions up to observation decks to gaze on the Michelin Tourbook Spectacular View only to find that when I got there I couldn't see a thing for the clouds, fog, rain or other disturbance that wasn't there when I started. If I had been along with Jesus when Satan took him up the pinnacle to show him the desires of the world there would have been no temptation—it would have been fogged in.

The message here is clear, even if this spectacular view is not. The meaningful and important thing is the journey. More of our lifetime is spent on getting there than on arriving, so it is important to make the journey as spectacular as you hope the arrival will be. Pay attention to the path, rather than only thinking how great the end is. Be here now, rather than concentrating on the future and merely grudgingly enduring the present.

Religious pietists who ignore the social, economic, and political problems and possibilities of the present and focus only on the alleged beauties of a life in heaven need to take note. I'm certain when we get there it will be fogged in.

"BE NOT AFRAID"

It is that time of year when people who have had loved ones die in hospitals and nursing homes begin to drift back to visit with staff. One thing is clear to those of us who have experienced death. We would like to cancel Christmas this year. With the persistent depression that permeates our being, the day is yet another obstacle to be endured, an inconvenient stumbling block on the way to what people tell us is "recovery." Shopping in gaily decorated stores, surrounded by familiar songs evoking warmth and pleasant memories is excruciatingly painful. Seeing things that we would get or do and then remembering with shock that he or she is not there to get or do for is jolting.

As we sit shaking, we do not want to hear the words of the angels to the shepherds: "Be not afraid." In the midst of feeling sad and angry, we do not want to hear "good news of great joy." As lonely darkness becomes ever more comfortable and secure, we do not wish to be disturbed to "see a great Light".

There is no room in the inn of our lives for this baby to be born in this way, in this place, at this time. We would prefer he come back later, a few months from now, a few years from now; come back when we want him—maybe not come back at all.

But here he is, this Jesus child, this holy squalling infant demanding to be heard. He comes, as is his custom, in the wrong place and at the wrong time, confronting fear with calm, ignoring grief with joyous mundane baby sounds, audaciously spilling Light, dispelling darkness.

He seems to know there is seldom room in the inn, if ever. And so he comes now into lives and worlds we claim are full, commanding us to hear and to see his presence as the present present God has given us. This Jesus child, this unwanted, untimely intrusion is even more persistent than the formerly fulfilling depression, even more pervasive, permeating our whole being.

And so, reluctantly, we once again go to Bethlehem to hear The Story, to be dragged kicking and screaming, just as this Child has been, into a rebirth of infancy, childhood, wonder and love. Perhaps the day will not be cancelled after all.

GOSPEL LITE

It was bad enough when J. B. Phillips completed his translation of the Bible and everyone called it "Phillips 66." (For the uninitiated, that is a joke because there are 66 books in the Bible.) Then came the abomination entitled "The Way," which is a paraphrased version. A group of folks disenchanted with the painstaking translations from Greek, Hebrew and Aramaic, sat down and decided what Jesus had *really* meant to say in English. I would paraphrase this version "no Way".

The best contender and unsurpassed winner in the Can You Top This? contest is the Reader's Digest Bible. This little jiffy is 40 percent shorter than the Revised Standard Version (Did they only put in 6 commandments?) Look at all the trees they saved.

By using the "three R's" as their guide (at least they're Trinitarian) they deleted all "repetition, rhetoric and redundancy." Well, it's about time somebody got all those wretched "begats" out of there and dumped the rhetoric so we can finally see what God is trying to tell us.

And don't expect your kids to recite the 23rd Psalm as you knew it. Because of streamlining and dropping many of the obviously unneeded psalms, 23 has become lucky #13. In addition, hundreds of what are termed "minor figures" have disappeared altogether. (How many times did you quote Biztha the Eunuch anyway?) Chronicles, Exodus and Deuteronomy (the ones with all the juicy stuff) were reduced 70%. The Gospels of Mark and Luke lost only 15% and 25%, respectively.

Treated somewhat more gingerly but not to be deleted from the deletions, are the words of Jesus which are reduced by 10%. Are we talking verbosity here? Maybe I will start doing "Lite" worship services. 70% fewer prayers, 10% less communion wine ("I came all the way down to the chapel and you do a *Lite* Service?")

The rationale for this travesty is to make the Bible "smoother, more inviting, more readable." That's exactly what many people have tried to do with religion for centuries—make it more palatable to the culture. The result is always watered down pablum mediocrity or worse.

The message of the Bible is consistently counter-culture. It is rough, confronting, demanding, reconciling, healing, forgiving, struggling. It is generally not palatable, inviting, smooth or readable.

I don't like The Reader's Digest Lite Bible. But, then, I also like my oatmeal lumpy and my coffee black. I wonder what Jesus thinks about being reduced 10%?

THE END IS NEAR

The other day someone asked me why clergy wear "those collars." The answer is "anachronism." A century ago *everyone* wore "those collars". Look at old pictures of the presidents and you'll see them clearly. Clergy being (at that time) generally conservative kept the old style as other styles changed. That means in 2083 we'll be wearing punk haircuts.

Wearing a collar is dangerous. It is amazing the effect a one-inch square of white material has on people. Public inebriates, whose vision usually fades beyond three feet, can spot it clearly at fifty paces. ("Hey, Faddah, gotta quatah ferra cuppa cawfee?") At the penitentiary where I was a chaplain, it was cause for daily verbal assaults from radical revolutionaries, well-read sociopaths, and disaffected Christians, all of whom sounded alike. My least favorite group of collar-spotters, though, are the Sunday-fundy-tribulationists; the folks who know the end of the world is coming and want to argue about it.

I was recently having lunch at a local place when the beeper went off. I took two steps to go to the pay phone and was stopped cold by the winner of the

Cowboys Linebacker Look-Alike Contest. The guy was big. He pointed to my collar and without so much as a howdy proceeded to ask me if I knew about prophecy. Well, he did too and when did I think the Tribulation was going to be?

It was on the tip of my tongue to say 4:30 this afternoon and have you got your stuff together with God, but the guy didn't have a sense of humour and you don't sass somebody when you're talking into their belt buckle. I did put my guardian angel to the test by saying, "I don't know. I don't care. And I don't believe it makes any difference anyway." Then I turned my back, walked toward the phone and waited for the screaming tackle. It never came. He was flabbergasted. I was lucky.

There have always been folks who believe the end is near and look forward to the disaster with diabolical glee. They expect the bad guys to suffer excruciating punishment while they and their peers slip off to heaven unscathed. It's like a Divine Neutron Bomb where only the Christians (of a particular belief) survive. By arguing with people about it now and convincing them of the upcoming disaster, souls are supposed to be scared into belief and salvation. Nice try, but did you ever hear of forgiveness and mercy?

The Biblical evidence for this happening is patently unclear. Jesus is more interested in living here and now than in concern about afterlife. Indeed, he doesn't seem to make much distinction between the two times. Equating current events with Revelation has been a favorite misleading pastime for centuries. Nobody knows when the world will end, and there are more important things to do than speculate about it. Feeding the hungry, working for social justice and preventing nuclear holocaust will do for openers.

I have always looked at it the other way around. Live now and if Jesus comes back consider it a stroke of luck. Until then we all still have to face car payments, meetings, and Mondays.

THE SECOND LETTER TO NATHAN

This is your second Christmas and it has fallen to me once again to explain it to you. Last year you were a bit too young to listen. (I still have the mashed carrot stains on my shirt from the occasion.) This year you are exercising an excellent command of the language with such words as "Chuck" and "car" and even some small sentences. Obviously, you are ready for the straight story now. So hang onto your diaper, kid; here it comes.

The first thing you should know is Christmas is not for kids. We are talking major drama here, Nate, not Mother Goose, so I'll break it down as best I can. It is an adult story involving procreation (I'll tell you about that later), poverty, governmental authority, rejection and the triumph of new life in spite of it all. If it were a movie it would be rated "R" at least. But you can understand the story because you see the adult themes through your child's eyes—an enviable combination.

Second, and I know this is hard to believe, Christmas is about *Jesus*. If you add up all the commercials on tv and in the papers with the songs on the radio, you'd think it was about buying and snow and reindeer and drinks and food and trees with fake snow. It is a celebration of Jesus' birthday, just like we do yours. You'd think we'd have balloons and cake and candles instead of that other stuff.

But we do have gifts, and that's something you already know a lot about. You give people gifts all the time: spoons and toys and pans and leaves and sticky food and books and smiles and laughs and sloppy kisses. And you generously allow us to give the same to you. You still have no sense of value, Nate. A wood pencil and a gold pen are the same to you, though they taste different. Maybe that's what it really means to give—no value but lots of taste. (Funny how Christmas gifts are often the opposite.)

It is a joyous time, Nathan, not just fun but joyous. We sing songs and eat and drink and sit around fires and tell lots of tales about Christmas past and hopes for our Christmas future. We show our gratefulness for God's gift to us of Jesus. And we show our gratefulness for God's gift to us now as symbolized in *you* tonight—new life, spontaneity, delight in vulnerability, openness to both pain and growth, willingness to love and give and share without regard to color or status.

What do you need to do to get ready, Nathan? Sleep and dream. Let images of a baby even smaller than yourself appear in your vast visions. See cows and sheep and horses and straw and a star so bright it lights the way for us all in the darkness.

Grow and learn. Play with that baby in the stable until you know who he is. Give to him. Take from him. Follow and watch what he does, with whom and to what ends. Laugh with him. Cry with him. Make up stories with him and let him make up your story with you.

Finally, Nathan, just be yourself. As you are to others, so we all are to God: childlike, free, hasty, demanding, creative, afraid, loving, imperfect, funny, loved. Just being you, you will be ready.

Just watching you, may we remember. And, in our remembering, may we let that baby be reborn in each of us this Christmas night.

Love,
Uncle Chuck

STRESS

No matter who you are, regardless of age, color, sex, national origin, religious belief or shoe size, there is one thing you are bound to experience again in this new year: Stress. A newpsaper interview recently deluged me with phone calls and letters for relaxation classes and tapes on stress. Stress is "in." It is in to have it and it is in to have theories about how to handle it.

As you might guess, the Bible has some salient comments on the subject as well. The following is the Biblical Approach to Stress, or BATS for short.

1 Kings 19:5 Here Elijah is encouraged to *rest, eat* and *exercise* as a way to handle his stressful journey. Self-nurturing in the most basic ways is affirmed as a method of handling the daily problems of our journey through life. (This is not to be confused with the one clear evidence of cannibalism in the Bible — 2 Kings 8:1).

2 Samuel 6:14 and 16 King David makes it obvious that *play* and dance are great stress-reducers. By this he does not intend the compulsive, determined, dogged approach where people work so hard at playing that they miss the point. Rather, he means the exuberance of the natural child within us laughing, exploring, dancing, playing with each other and with God.

Ephesians 4:26 The Apostle Paul tells us it's normal to have negative feelings and offers a way to handle them. *"Be angry but do not sin;* do not let the sun go down on your anger."* Rather than let stress build up over feelings, go to the person now, be honest and explain the problem, express your anger or frustration and then (vv.31-32) be forgiving and get on with your lives.

Matthew 6:34 Jesus suggests that we *"be not anxious about tomorrow."* He knew that many people waste their entire lives worrying about the future and feeling guilty, angry, sad or resentful about the past. He also knew that the only time we have to live is today and that the more we focus on and stay in the here and now the more control, responsibility and power we have and the less stress we feel.

I would encourage you to check out these references for yourself and experiment with following them as a stress management technique. And if anyone catches you flipping through your Bible, just tell them you're religiously going BATS.

PERFECT

Nobody's perfect. That's why God created erasers, spell-check, and forgiveness. And yet I constantly hear supposedly religious people demanding perfection of themselves and others, judging themselves (and especially others) harshly for falling short of some imagined state of impeccability.

It is as though we believe that unless we constantly, everywhere, all the time measure up to what we are told Jesus was like we will be forever denied entrance into heaven and spend our guilt-ridden immortality someplace that makes Laredo in August seem like Fairbanks in February.

As usual the source of such pious foolishness is a misquote of Jesus. In Matthew 5.40 he says: "You, therefore, must be perfect, as your heavenly Father is perfect." Now this may come as a shock but the New Testament was not originally written in King James English and the Greek word for *perfect* really means *mature* or *whole*.

To be mature or whole carries for me the connotation of balance. It means to have feelings, all kinds of feelings, joy and depression, anger and sorrow, love and hate. It means to have all kinds of thoughts, pleasant and scary, hopeful and dreadful, selfish and giving. It means to express these thoughts and feelings, to integrate them and balance them in relationships with others who are thinking and feeling the same things we are.

To be whole as Jesus meant it implies admitting and accepting our imperfection and recognizing with humility our need for each other in this fragile world family. To be mature is to treat people fairly even when we know they don't deserve it; it is to be just in an unjust world; it is to allow others to love us when we know we are unlovable. As Christians we are called *not* to be perfect—just different.

And as for assuming that the striving for perfection is a guarantee of earned eternal life and immortality, there is plenty of Biblical evidence to indicate that entrance into heaven is a gift that can never be earned, bought or deserved. Rather we would do well to follow the words of a 5th century Greek quoted by Camus: "O my soul, do not aspire to immortal life; But exhaust the limits of the possible."

Imperfect wholeness is possible.

MISQUOTES

The Bible is probably the most widely misquoted document in the world. Everybody who has seen "King of Kings," "The 10 Commandments" or "The Robe" thinks they can quote it accurately. Most of what people quote, however, is hearsay from Hollywood. The following are examples of THINGS THAT AREN'T IN THE BIBLE.

The three wise men. A popular trivia question is to name the three wise men. Most people think their names were Balthazar, Gaspar and Melchior. They are only mentioned in Matthew 2 and nowhere is their exact number stated. Their names and number were made popular through the Christmas hymn and the wonderful if inaccurate pageants and creches.

The patience of Job. Anyone who attributes "patience" to the main character in the book of Job simply hasn't read it lately. Job does not sit around and wait to be vindicated. After listening to the affronts of his alleged friends, he repeatedly asserts the case for his integrity. He constantly reminds God of God's covenant with him and argues (in the style of a lawyer) for his vindication (See especially chapter 31.) One might better describe this attitude as "the self-confidence of Job."

Jonah and the whale. Walt Disney strikes again. Folks who believe this also think that Jiminey Cricket and Pinnochio were in there with him. Almost every culture, especially in the Ancient Near East, has its story of a man being swallowed up by an animal and living to tell about it. In the case of the Bible the scene was adapted to fit the particular story the people had to tell. The Hebrew actually reads "dag gathol" meaning "big fish". Probably it was a minnow that got nuked.

The Lord helps those who help themselves. I used to hear this one a lot at the penitentiary, for obvious reasons. ("Hey, man, I was just helpin' myself.") It is also used as a justification for everything from working hard in school or jobs to stubbornly maintaining independence in the face of debilitating illness. While it may be a useful axiom, it is not found in the Bible. It comes from the same genius that brought us Daylight Savings Time: Ben Franklin, in *Poor Richard's Almanac.*

The point for me is to be very careful of confusing popular images with the real stories and descriptions in the Bible. Often the Bible is used to support a popular cultural belief that has nothing to do with the Judaeo-Christian ethic.

I recommend reading it for yourself. The book really is a lot better than the movie.

A DONKEY NAMED GLORY

(Nathan Brown Joslin is a two-year-old friend of mine.)

Dear Nathan:

Once upon a time in a land far away a man and a woman came to an inn. The woman might have looked a lot like your mama and the man had a beard like your papa and worked with wood like he does too. The woman was about to have a baby and they had no place to stay. The innkeeper asked them to wait outside until he could see if there was room in the small barn. He went out back and saw the animals all snug in their stalls. He told them *they* would have to decide whether this couple could sleep there. One of the animals would have to give up its place if the couple came in. There simply was not room for them all.

The chicken spoke up first. She clucked indignantly, "Well *I* certainly can't be expected to give up *my* nest to some, some *humans*, for goodness sake. I have a family to look after, foxes to watch out for and responsibilities to maintain. And that's that." She jerked her head and closed her beady eyes.

"Don't be so hard boiled, Sadie," said the slow talking cow in the next stall. "You know you'll feel better if you let them in. Be a little more liberal with your space. You've got more than you need. *I*, on the other hand, *have* to stay here. People depend on me to give them fresh milk in the morning. If I freeze up, people won't have anything nutritious to drink. (Smoothies hadn't been invented yet, Nate.) I'm too important to society to give up *my* place to some ordinary humans." She batted her long eyelashes at the innkeeper and swished her tail at a fly.

"How 'bout you, Oinker?" the man said to the mud-covered pig at the end.

"Me? How about *Me?* You have *got* to be kidding!" he sloshed in the thick mud and fell on his face. "I'm not even worth asking. Nobody'd want anything from *me*. Nobody'd want to sleep in *this* mess but a pig. I'm disgusting. I'm dirty, my stall isn't good enough for them." He buried his head in the mud so only his squiggly tail pointed out. "No, no, no. It's too humiliating. I couldn't think of it."

"Well, I don't suppose there's any point in asking *you*, is there, Stoney?" the man said to the old mule lying down in her stall.

Ask me what?" she said, sarcastically.

"Ask you if this young couple can have your stall. You're so fat and stubborn I can hardly get you out of it in the middle of summer, much less on a cold night like tonight." He turned to go. "Okay. I'll tell them there's no room in the barn either. Guess she'll have to have her baby out in..."

"Wait a minute, wait a minute." Stoney said. "What's your hurry?" The old mule struggled to her feet, breathing heavily. "Come over here and unlock the gate to this stall."

The chicken's head jerked around, her eyes popping open with a loud "Cluck!" The cow stopped chewing her cud and the straw dropped out of her mouth. The pig popped his head out of the slop and shook the dripping mud off his nose. They all watched, wide-eyed, as Stoney ambled out of her warm stall into the cold, starry night.

A few minutes later the bearded man helped his very pregnant wife slowly make her way into the barn. The animals felt bad that they had been so selfish with their comfortable homes. They heard the sigh of relief when the woman lay down in the warm straw of Stoney's stall. Still thinking about the old mule and listening to the comforting murmurs of the bearded man, they all fell into a troubled sleep.

Just at daybreak, the silence of the early morning was shattered by a cry. The cow opened one large, brown eye. The pig jumped awake and fell over in the mud. The chicken's feathers ruffled in surprise. All three tiptoed to Stoney's stall to see the young couple holding a newborn baby wrapped in old rags. Just at that moment the barn door flew open and the innkeeper appeared holding in his arms a brand new baby donkey, shivering from the cold.

"Bring him in here where it's warm," the woman said. And the innkeeper carefully laid the baby donkey in the straw beside the human baby.

"What are their names?" asked the pig.

Suddenly there appeared in the stall a beautiful angel surrounded by a radiant light. The angel said: "The baby boy's name is `Jesus.' The baby donkey is to be called `Glory.' And these two babies will grow up to meet again on a road outside Jerusalem, where hundreds of people will welcome them into that great city with palms."

"But where is Stoney?" the cow asked, looking around the barn.

The innkeeper looked very sad. "Stoney, uh, didn't make it," he said.

The angel, in a soft voice that comforted and consoled them, said, "Stoney gave her life so that others could live. Her spirit is with me now. Please remember her by living that way too." Then, in a second, the angel vanished.

There was a long silence while everyone thought about Stoney and the angel. Then both at the same time, the baby cried and the little donkey opened its eyes and stood up on its scrawny, wobbly legs, only to plop right down again in the hay. Even though everyone felt sad about Stoney, they couldn't help laughing at the two babies. (New life always calls our attention from death, Nate.)

Finally, as the morning sun sliced through the boards in the old barn walls, the animals huddled around the stall to keep warm. The baby Jesus gawked at all the strange faces staring at him, and Glory nuzzled up to Jesus' face and licked it with his rough tongue which was his way of saying "Glory to Jesus." And people have been saying it ever since that first Christmas Day.

Love,

Uncle Chuck

SHUTTLE MEMORIAL

January 31, 1985

We do not want to be here in this Chapel today. Yet, here we are. We tried not to come. We made up excuses, but the excuses were not good enough to keep us away. Reluctantly, we made our way here together: embarrassed, confused, angry, stunned. And here we sit, wondering why we are here at all, wondering what can be said that would make any difference, yet needing desperately to be here, to be somewhere, to be with others who are feeling as we do.

What *are* we doing here? We are here because we feel sad. We are here because we have been touched. We are here because we don't know what else to do.

Sadness. The death of a dream. A rude awakening to the laws of physics. Expectations exploded in a perfect blue sky. Eyes blinded by a fatal flash of red. Hopes of millions reduced to dust and smoke. Headlines become obituaries.

Touched. The scene indelibly etched into our memories. Like Pearl Harbor, J.F.K., Robert Kennedy,

Martin Luther King, Jr. We will remember where we were when we saw or heard it. We will remember the people, the feelings, the horror, the disbelief. We will remember her. Teacher. Citizen. One of us. You. Me. It could have been us up there. Indeed, it *was* us up there. We are touched because we *know* that, because we *were* there, and because that part of us is gone forever.

We don't know what else to do. Like an old house in a bad dream, nothing works. We know people die every day. We know they die in far away unseen places of starvation and terrorism and torture and ignorance. We know they die close by of disease and heartbreak and accident and decision. We know we are not in total control—but we are not used to such a graphic, terrifying reminder.

We try to see it logically, but logic fails to help. We want to get over this, to feel complete again, to recompose our shattered worlds. But we feel stuck, overwhelmed, confused, lost. And so we come here. Together. Hoping someone among us will know how to help us start again. And it is in *coming* here that we *have* started.

The basis for hope is memory. We come, not to help each other forget, but to help each other remember. We come to convince each other to dream again even in the face of death. We come to convince each other to ignore again the laws of physics and reach beyond our grasp. We come to hold each other while we risk opening our squinting eyes again to the blinding light of the future. We come to resurrect our hopes out of the ashes, dust and smoke of disaster and boldly build them up again with the mortar of memory.

What will we do? We will keep on being. Again aware of the fragility of life, we will take our sadness and allow it to remind us to live our lives fully here and now; we will take our sense of being touched and allow ourselves to continue to be vulnerable with one another; we will take our sense of not knowing what to do and let it grow again into trust. Our common memory will not permit us to do less than to hope.

In a little while, we will go on. But we will not be the same. We are all older now. With one more thing to remember.

GOD WINKS BACK

(Vacation journal notes.)

I don't like church. As I sit here in this beautiful cathedral in Limburg, that is the first thought that crosses my mind. The contrast between this 600 year-old building and the unimaginative pre-fab boxes in which we worship at home is remarkable. The gold and wood crucifix suspended over the ancient altar is bathed in color from the rose window in the west transept. The carved wood pulpit clings to a stone pillar in the *center* of the congregation, taking the Word into the *midst* of the people, not handing it down from up front. The dusky sweet smell of incense wafts up past the fading frescoes that depict saints being saints and sinners being sinners.

The old Germans knew what they were doing. Their theology was graphic, even blatant, and the stone masons, painters and architects made sure those beliefs were built into their places of worship. A stained glass window depicts for an illiterate populace Bible stories in blues and greens. A hungry beast of Hell with sharpened fangs and tongue of fire devours the hopeless as they frantically cry for deliverance. That sight alone is enough to make me want to be good—at least until next vacation.

It is easy to worship here. One has a sense of being overwhelmed in this edifice. The immense space reminds us of our smallness in the grand scheme of things: we and God are put in our proper places. The age of the place is also overpowering. It has stood in the same position since the world was flat, rats plagued its people, the town was lost and won to ever new invaders, industrial revolution fouled its river, scoured its exterior and employed its people, Reichs rose and bombs fell, nuclear arms were placed within sight of its ever watchful steeple. Time means as little as personalities in here. Contrary to American churches where charisma builds following, the clergy here are nearly invisible. It is hard to be anything but anonymous in a place that has preceded you by 600 years and will, hopefully, witness the deaths of your great-grandchildren.

But lest the sense of time and space pommel us into insignificance, the Germans wink at God. It is hard to be pious in a place that has, built into the very pillars, faces of ridiculous people with their eyes crossed and tongues stuck out; pigs and cows with menacing smiles, gargoyles of unknown animal parentage with foolish grins and missing teeth. In the midst of being overwhelmed, one smiles. In the midst of sin and guilt there is comic relief. In the overpowering presence of God, there is a redeeming sense of humour.

Maybe if American churches took themselves with less piety and more humility, I'd feel more worshipful there. Maybe if they were both as boldly overwhelming and ridiculously silly as this cathedral, I'd feel at home in them.

It is important to remember that German sense of balance in our religion and in our lives. If we maintain that, I think we will find that God winks back.

NAME CHANGE

I love words. I am fascinated by their sights and sounds, their imagery and their power. John Steinbeck was able to tell exactly where in America a person lived just by hearing him/her talk. He lamented the loss of regional language and the capitulation to bland t.v. speech that always sounds the same. I enjoy hearing the people in my life nonchalantly reveal their origins. I love to hear Laura Lowy say "ayaple" ("apple"), Dana Joslin say "wheel" ("will"), Adele Lorusso say "Foat Wuth," and the Southern twang of Kathy and Gep on the overhead paging system saying anything at all. We live daily amidst a symphony of sounds surrounding us with special persons from unique places.

Words can also be used to cover up unpleasantries or deliberately avoid reality. The Pentagon has decreed that the word "killing" is to be replaced in its documents with "unlawful or arbitrary deprivation of life." "Civilian casualties in nuclear war" are to be referred to as "collateral damage." And (are you ready for this?) the word "peace" is to be called "permanent pre-hostility." Another agency has replaced the term "plane crash" with "uncontrolled flight into terrain."

Healthcare words do the same thing. Journal articles refer to newborns as "genetically anomalous," "defective" (like a bad car?), and "handicapped" (by whose standards?) Death is changed to "passed away," "lost," or "expired" (like a library card or parking meter?) Worst of all, as healthcare begins to be seen as an "industry," articles are referring to the patient as "product," and services as "product lines."

In the Bible, words are extremely important. The Hebrews believed that saying someone's name impled complete knowledge of that person. Thus, when they saw the name "God" in the Torah, they read "Lord," so as not to imply that they completely understood the Unfathomable. Contrast this with Jesus who consistently calls God "Abba" or "Daddy." The images are powerful and lasting.

What we call ourselves, think about ourselves, see when we look in the mirror in the morning, is important in the same way. If we refer to ourselves or to our work or family in negative ways, negative images result. If we believe we are basically unacceptable, unloved, unworthy, we will act in such a manner as to have those things become true. If we believe our work or our family is unsupportive, meaningless, antagonistic, we will arrange for it to appear that way.

God and Jesus repeatedly show their interest in words and names throughout the Old and New Testaments. And they consistently change words and names to conform with Truth. They call war war and peace peace. They berate those who "cry peace, peace when there is no peace." They call death death and lepers lepers. They talk of healing, forgiveness and love in ways that are unashamedly straightforward and blunt.

Most importantly, they change the names of people (Jacob, Simon, Saul, you and me) from mere objects to growing, changing beings. They constantly show that people are more than the positions they hold, the diseases they have, the number on the census, the name on the time card. And in this changing we are freed from the boundaries set upon us and that we set upon ourselves.

Imagine for a moment what would happen if you let God change your name from the one you know to the one God knows is the real you, if you let God whisper that name in your ear, let it wash over and inside you, making you new and whole. Then look in the mirror and see who's there.

And see what language you begin to speak.

LESSONS FROM MICHAL

For the past few months I have been interacting with my seven year old daughter-to-be, Michal. It is one thing to begin a new phase of life with someone your own age, but it is entirely something else to do so with a child. And since my experience with small human beings has been a little to the right of W.C. Fields, suffice it to say it is a whole new world out there.

Fortunately, I lucked out. This one is so sweet I may soon be going for daily blood sugar checks. Even the awkward moments are thought provoking. She has acquainted me with Rainbow Brite, Star Fillies, Pipi Longstocking, and Little Miss Make-Up. And I have taught her such useful phrases as "gotta make a pit stop', "ding dong brain", "a shot of milk, please", and other equally delicate expletives about which her mother is, naturally, ecstatic.

Also for the past few months, I have been confronted with friends from across the country informing me of various kinds of change in their lives, from sickness, death, and divorce, to job changes, career moves, adoptions and late life baby birthing. Is it the mid-life fabulous forties, the harmonic convergence, or the quick shifting to get into a secure position before the president leaves and Someone New takes his place? I don't know, but all these events did begin to make sense after Michal got sick last weekend.

She went to school Thursday and came home with a virus that wouldn't quit, a fever like Brownsville in August, and tonsils the size of watermelons, and as red. We ended up having an unpleasant time in a hospital emergency room where Michal, under extreme fever and impossible odds, managed to wake everyone from here to the Pacific when five people in white entered the small room and quickly plunged a needle into her small, restrained arm. Sick people waiting outside miraculously became well and vanished. Ambulances turned around and went elsewhere. Opera agents lined up behind the door. There was nothing wrong with her lungs.

It occurred to me, standing over her, holding her face in my direction so she would not watch the event (and wondering if my hearing would ever return) that this is exactly how many of us handle change. We live our lives blithely thinking we will escape it, expecting things to go along pretty much the same as always, shocked and unprepared, even when we have had a lifetime of experience to the contrary, for the pain of that metaphoric needle plunging deep into our arm, at which time we scream "NOOOOOOOOOOOOOOOOO!!"

It is as though we are outraged at the pain which inevitably accompanies change, incensed at this unwarranted intrusion into our lives, angered at the audacity of life-changing events, depressed by the decisions we must make from seemingly unlimited options, or from options which are far too limited. We seem constantly surprised that life keeps coming at us from different directions, bringing change, loss, renewal—birth, death, resurrection. We act as though change is optional, that the normal order of things is static, that the choices are between pain and no pain.

The truth is that change is the only certainty with which we live. It sometimes is seen far off, as in long terminal illnesses and national elections (which are a lot alike). Even in those times, when change is known and anticipated, it is usually not fully realized until it actually happens, at which time we act as though it was a complete surprise. More often, however, change hits us as that horrifying shot in the arm did Michal—from nowhere.

In either case, the choice that change demands of us is never between pain and no pain. It is always between which pain we prefer: the pain of remaining where we are, or the pain of moving into the new.

Michal could choose the pain of staying sick or the pain of getting well (involving a needle the size of a pipeline). People can chose the pain of staying in unhealthy relationships (jobs, towns, families, religions,) or the pain of breaking from them; the pain of holding onto anger, or the pain of expressing it; the pain of repeating old psychological patterns, or the pain of therapeutically confronting them; the pain of security or the pain of risk.

Jesus' words were clear: give it up, don't look back, risk everything, move on down the road, leave the dead to bury the dead, keep on truckin', happiness is Lubbock in your rearview mirror, and the cotton ball taped onto your arm where the needle used to hurt.

Often, as Jesus also knew, we need help from friends to get through these times, whether they are lowering us down through the roof tiles on a pallet, or holding us on a white gurney as we scream our lungs out, or listening for the thousandth time to the hurt that still stings, or telling us the truth about ourselves, or making us laugh again.

Thank you, Michal, for yet another reminder of who we are.

I wonder what delicate new phrase I can teach you in return?

WAITING

While making rounds in the hospital the other day, it suddenly dawned on me what it is that people do more than anything else.

They *wait*.

They *wait* for tests, they *wait* for test results, they *wait* for meals, they *wait* for physician visits, they *wait* (impatient patients) for their bodies to heal, they *wait* for visitors, they *wait* for baths, medications, i.v.'s to be started or removed, they *wait* to go home, they *wait* to die.

And each of us, in our own worlds, does the same thing. We wait in the supermarket to check out, we wait in the hotel line to check in, we wait in restaurants to be served, we wait at the Post Office, the bank, the bakery. (And we know it is a fundamental rule of the universe that whatever line we choose will turn out to be the l-o-n-g-e-s-t one.) We wait for payday, for vacation, for the weekend. We wait for mail, for the phone to ring, for the other shoe to drop. We wait for traffic lights to change, for seasons to change, for political administrations to change, for people to change.

We teach our children to do the same thing. They wait for their turn, they wait for us to get them at child care (and hope not to be the last one picked up.) They wait for school to be out, for summer to get here, to go to Sea World, to visit relatives, to see friends, for summer to be over, to go back to school. They wait for their parents to understand them, or to get off their case (if they are adolescents.) They (can't) wait to grow up, at which time they wait for all the things mentioned in the preceding paragraph.

You can tell a lot about someone by the way they wait. In the hospital, they read old magazines, pretending to be interested in the news of the week for February 12, 1984. They watch T.V., pretending to be entertained by what barely passes for plot and acting (except for Dallas, of course.) They watch videos, write letters, time the passing of hours by medications, think about the meaning of their hospitalization, worry about everything from bills to disability.

Some of us hum as we wait in lines, others read the National Enquirer or gawk at the latest gorgeous faces on the front of the magazines at the check out counters. Some people wait with anger, some with boredom, some with equanimity.

In contrast to all our usual passivity, the Gospel stories tell us about 'creative waiting." Rather than just passing time until something better comes along to attract our attention, we are told to "ask," "seek," "knock," "question," "give," "clothe," "feed," "visit." Creative waiting is not optimistic; it is hopeful. It is a way of waiting without regard for reward or outcome. It is a way to focus entirely on the present, living *now* instead of in the past or the future. It is an acknowledgement that we never wait alone, even in our times of silent introspection.

As we wait for the summer heat to break, school to start, wait for the many activities of Fall to begin, there are two sayings that may be useful to remember. The first is from the penitentiary where I worked. There, the inmates said: "Fun flies when you're doing time." The second is a poster in a friend's office: "Life is what you do while you are waiting to die."

May we wait creatively together, actively living our days with a balance of enjoyment and service.

LIFE IS A JOURNEY

Metaphors are meaningful. We live our lives by them. The images we use to describe our experiences are powerful determinants of the way we feel, act and respond. Often the metaphors for who we are are based on heros we emulated as children, adolescents, or adults. If we see ourselves as John Wayne, for instance, we will probably have a very different life experience than if our internal metaphor (picture of who we are) is that of Ghandi, or King, or Mother Theresa, or Cyndi Lauper, or Cher.

Jesus used metaphors all the time. He described the Kingdom of Heaven as a mustard seed, a wedding feast, a thief in the night, and a pearl of great price. In the last few weeks, I've heard some equally interesting descriptions about life that seem worth sharing.

Life is a river.—This metaphor conjures up a picture of water flowing inevitably forward at its own pace, unable to be either hurried or impeded. Sometimes there are rapids, floods, or undertows, but the movement is ultimately downstream into the ocean of the universe. The problem with this metaphor is that it is directed, confined and limited by its banks (or in the case of the U.S., its S&L's.) Persons embracing this metaphor usually "go with the flow."

Life is a mountain.—A particular favorite of mystics from Dante to Tolkien to Merton, this goal oriented picture is one of a strenuous journey upward toward a high pinnacle. One may encounter any number of interesting events, persons, or creatures on the way to the ultimate goal of reaching the top and becoming one with the universe, or meeting a wise old person who will provide The Answer to all of one's questions. Unfortunately, The Answer may turn out to be: "Life is a river."

Life is a beach.—Why do all these images have to do with vacation spots? Since most of our time is spent at our place of employment, why don't we have some realistic work metaphors? Why can't someone say "Life is an expressway at rush hour," or "Life is like buffing the floors," or "Life is like scraping cafeteria trays," or "Life is a parking garage." Actually, life is not a beach. The only reason people say that is to avoid saying "Life is like a canine of the female persuasion, and then you die—if you're lucky."

Life is a mystery.—Berdyaev (a Russian theologian) said "Life is not a problem to be solved, but a mystery to be lived," which probably helped him through daily life in the Soviet Union. Adherents to this image accept that not everything has an answer, that there may not be reasons for events, or even a definable purpose for existence. While this one makes some sense to me,

I keep thinking that, given enough time, Sherlock would figure it out.

Life is a journey.—This metaphor has a much more interactive feel to it. One is not simply a pawn, but a responsible companion, even co-creator with Life. On this journey, one may travel over and through rivers, up and down mountains, lie on beaches, and accept that there are things he or she will never comprehend. No matter how long, it is a short journey for the traveler, involving physical strength, emotional dilemmas and spiritual mysteries. Above all, it is a journey of *risk*. There are unknowns (both dangers and surprises) in every decision. Every decision matters, just as one foot put in front one the other determines our direction. And yet, there is a sense in which the journey is playful, reminding us to take ourselves with a large grain of humour, knowing where all our paths must end—at the start of another journey.

Life is a journey, not a destination. And, sometimes, when it seems like a canine, it is important to remember that the point is not whether we have reached the elusive goal, but how well we have traveled.

LIFE IS GIFT

In the previous piece I believed that "Life is a journey." And that is true. On this journey we experience wonderful surprises, devastating disappointments, expected and unexpected pleasures, excruciating pain and loneliness, giggly laughter, fierce anger, immobilizing fear and empowering love. But the events of the past few weeks have reminded me that life is something else also: A dear friend whom I love is diagnosed with cancer and has six months to live; a two year old baby hangs himself on a toy necklace; one friend has a seizure and another must have surgery repeated and risks paralysis again; a seventeen year old only daughter is killed in a car wreck, in which another friend's daughter is seriously injured; an entire family is wiped out in a car wreck; a well loved local boy dies of leukemia; a woman finds out at 28 weeks she has a baby that is "incompatible with life;" political hostages are brutally murdered, airplane engines fall out of the sky and hundreds are killed in runway crashes; and a brilliant, funny, creative young man commits suicide. By last Friday I was telling everyone to get tragedies in by 5PM, as we would not be accepting any more this year after the deadline. Unfortunately, one or two more made it just under the wire. It seems as though the Harmonic Convergence is coming unglued.

What then, shall we say to this? There are several options. We could say that all life is suffering and the only sensible response is to escape to Nirvana through any means at our disposal, and there are many. Or, with the New Age people, we could say that the universe is metamorphosing, punishing us for our disrespect and pollution of it. With the cynics, we could look for the worst and hope for the best, being surprised by neither. Or, with the happy faced Smurfs, we could look for some unknown, overriding good in all of this tragedy. Finally, with the Sunday Fundys we could presume the Will of God is in fact behind all this sadness, bringing forth God's Perfect Plan And Purpose for each of the lives of the suffering or dead victims and their devastated survivors.

While each of these options may work for a while, none is really satisfying. As Whitehead said, "There is ultimately no comfort in a lie."

The truth is, as I see it from a Christian perspective, that life is more than a journey: Life is *gift*. It comes unexpected and undeserved. We didn't ask to be born (as adolescents remind parents daily). We don't get what we deserve (and it is, most often, a good thing), and we most certainly do not deserve what we get.

Gifts come wrapped. Life is wrapped with experiences, feelings, explorations, loves, disappointments, titles, successes, failures, clothes, possessions, deep and lasting attachments to people and things and places. But the gift is more than the wrapping, even though the wrapping is an integral part of the gift, giving it its color, its depth, its emotion. And it is my attachment to that wrapping that makes me so furiously angry when the wrapping, the colors, the specific body of personality, is randomly discarded by disability and death.

Gifts are free. Life cannot be purchased or grabbed or demanded. It is free gift. There are no strings in terms of conditions for receiving it, or in terms of the Giver, marionette like, controlling it. The Giver gives the gift and then both rejoices and deeply suffers with us as we live it, without external intervention. And here lies the problem. We want life to be fair, to make sense, to be just. But a free gift is none of these things. A free gift is free. And it is as free to be affected by insidious mental and physical disease processes and cars out of control and terrorist bombs as it is free to be affected by deep loving relationships and Nobel prizes, and sacrifice for one another, and forgiveness and mercy and care.

Gifts are durable and fragile. Life presents us with occasions for strength, support and enduring love. And yet life is easily broken beyond repair, before we're through admiring the gift, playing with it, turning it around and seeing it from all angles.

When that happens, we call it death, tragedy, untimely loss. We feel angry, disappointed, furious at the unfairness of events, the lack of control over circumstances. And we know that the gift cannot be fixed. It cannot be made whole again, the illness taken away, the body cleansed of disease or the suicide decision undone, taken back or changed.

But it is the Christian belief that, though our lives cannot be fixed, they can be healed; though we cannot undo what has happened, we can forgive and be forgiven; though we cannot make sense out of hostile, unjust circumstances, we can redeem those situations. In fact it is death, the loss of the free gift, that calls us to do exactly these things.

When presented with the inevitable tragedies and unfairness of our lives and the lives of those we love, we are supposed to recoil in anger because of our inevitable attachment to the wrapping; then we are to use the energy behind that anger to band together, to help however we can, to be present in difficult times for the victims and survivors, to use the time we have left to heal the tearing that the tragedy has caused, and to heal even in the face of impending death, for death and healing are often one.

Lastly, gifts are to be remembered; for the basis of hope is memory. In times of deep sadness, we remember the gift of each other, the importance of our interdependence, the truth that within our community of faith, we are not alone. So our response to tragedy must end in further commitment to serving, deeper attachment to the wrapping of each other, clearer vision of the path we are on, and a renewed willingness to take the risk of involvement once again.

Finally, we go out from here with a sense of thankfulness for this day of our gift of life together. For it is the only one we really know we have.

PLACE MAPS

Every morning my daughter, Michal, and I sit at the breakfast table and quiz each other on state capitols. Actually *she* quizzes *me* by eating her cereal and gazing at her place mat which has the states and the capitols in living color. (*MY* place mat has numbers and bears on it.) I'll bet you can ask me any capital and I'll know it, except possibly New Jersey or West Virginia or Wisconsin.

Anyway, that got me to thinking about maps and our perspective on things. When I was getting married a few months ago, my then-fiancee asked me to draw a map for our relatives to get to our houses from the airport. I spent an hour meticulously drawing the streets, interstate, exits, and landmarks involved in getting from the airport to my house, her house, the church, and the hotel. Things were carefully labeled, with appropriate arrows showing the fastest routes to the destinations. After I had mailed the copies, she looked at the paper and was completely lost.

North was at the bottom of the map. South was at the top. East was on the west side and west on the east side. Even though the N-S-E-W arrows were clearly drawn, it looked as though the only way you could find the various places was if you were standing on your head in the car.

What we eventually figured out was that the map was drawn as if the center of the universe was my chair at my desk in my study in my house. It became clear (the only thing that *was* clear) that I had drawn the map entirely from my own personal perspective.

And there is a lesson in that—for that is how we generally approach life, is it not? When someone asks us about religion, politics, art, child raising, hospital care, or the ethics of withdrawing artificial interventions, we respond with a point of view that observes the universe from our particular point in it. And when we greet someone new, don't we usually respond as though our standards are the ones by which to judge *their* behavior, clothes, beliefs?

Now the point here is not to invalidate our individual perceptions. We may, in fact, have developed some truths about existence that are worth passing along. That is why, in nearly every culture but our own, the elderly are held in high esteem, for their experience and wisdom of years. And, after all, the map did get people where they were supposed to go— once they were oriented to it.

But the truth is that there are *many* perspectives from which to view life. That map I drew could have been drawn from many views: from my fiancee's house, from the airport as the center, or from the Capitol (which, for those of you without place mats, is Austin.)

And the interesting thing is that ALL of those perspectives are CORRECT and proper. Any one of them will get you where you're going. And before judging someone else's directions to be inaccurate, it is wise to orient to their point of view. Many paths—same mountain.

So the next time I draw a map, I will be careful to get input from other people and to design it from the most helpful perspective, not just from mine alone, and to realize that there are more views of the universe (and of West Virginia, New Jersey and Wisconsin) than mine—all of which have their value. Because the important thing is not to criticize each other's path; the important thing is to help each other get where we're going.

A STAR NAMED TINK

(Nathan Brown Joslin is a three-year-old friend of mine.)

Dear Nathan:

In previous years I began your letters, "My Dear Little Nathan." I cannot do that any more. You are far from "little." In fact, I had my first real phone conversation with you last week. You were so excited about climbing Enchanted Rock without falling down even once! You've come a long way from the stewed carrots on my shirt. Now we play squirt guns and chase each other and do silly things to make each other laugh.

But some responsibilities remain the same, Nate, and it is my lot (as the alleged Family Theologian) to go on explaining Christmas to you each year. Next year you will probably be reading it for yourself, so I decided to save the heavy duty stuff until then. For now, let me tell you about a star.

Do you remember being out camping with your Papa and lying on your back at night and looking up into the sky? And do you remember what you saw up there? That's right, Nathan. Stars. Millions of stars. And although they seem to change with the seasons, we know that they are all in the same place every night.

Well, it didn't used to be that way. In fact, a long, long time ago there weren't as many stars as there are today. The world was a lot smaller then and didn't need as many to keep the sky dotted at night. (There were also a lot more fireflies, and that helped). And the stars were not fixed in their positions then, either. Back then, every night the Chief Star—who was the oldest and the wisest star in all the heavens—would line up all the other stars and assign them their posts for the night.

He knew exactly where the different kinds of light were needed. He would send the Bright Bright Stars, who were usually a little older and more experienced, to the most difficult and important places. He would send the Shiny Stars, who were still learning but had been at their jobs a while, to light up places that required lots of skill and intelligence. To the other positions in the night sky, the Chief Star would send the Plain Stars, who were young and still in training. Then, if there were any places left over, or any of the others needed some help, the Chief Star would, with some reluctance, call up the Little Stars and send them off.

The Little Stars, as you have probably guessed, were the smallest, the youngest and the least experienced of all. In stars' age, Nathan, they were even a few months younger than you. Sometimes they would fall, or drop something and break it, or skin their points, or spill their milkshake, or forget where they left their socks, or do something that wasn't nice and have to have a "time out" in their room. Most of the time, though, they were very cooperative and wanted to learn their job and grow up to do it well.

One night, a long, long time ago, the Chief Star had made all his assignments. It was a very deep night and he had to send out nearly every available star so that only a few of the Little Stars were left. He had just filled the last position in the sky with the very last Plain Star, when suddenly a Shooting Star whooshed up to him with an emergency message! The message read: "URGENT! Need Bright Bright Star over Bethlehem stable, immediately! HURRY!"

Well the Chief Star was horrified. Of all times for such an emergency to occur! What could he do? How could he meet the need with only the smallest and youngest and most inexperienced stars left to send? So he thought and thought, but the more he thought the more time passed and the more anxious he got. Then, just as he was about to pick the biggest of the Little Stars, he felt a tug on one of his points. It was Tink, the youngest of the Little Stars, who was just about your age.

"What do *you* want?" the Chief Star said gruffly.

"I want to help, Mr. Chief Star," Tink said in a squeaky little voice.

The Chief Star laughed and all the other Little Stars did too. How could Tink help? How could he possibly think that he could handle this job?

"I know I can do it, Mr. Chief Star. I *know* I can."

The Chief Star leaned over and patted Tink on his point. "That's very kind of you, Tink. But this is beyond your abilities. Even the oldest of the Little Stars will not be able to provide enough light for this assignment. You go back and wait until...."

"But I *can* do it! Just give me a chance," Tink said. "I am *very* brave, and I am *very* smart. I'll think of something." He looked over his shoulder. "Besides, nobody else wants to go."

The Chief Star saw the other Little Stars cowering in the background and knew time was running out. He would have to send this insignificant, inexperienced, not very bright Little Star. There was nothing else to do.

"Okay, Tink. Here are the directions to Bethlehem. I'll probably get fired for this, but you're the only thing I've got." The Chief Star pointed the way. "You'll have to hurry, though."

Tink knew it was a long way to go, but he had no idea how long it would take. He had to run very fast and peddle his bike faster than ever before and swim through the entire Milky Way with all his strength, and dodge flying meteors and watch out for comets hurtling out of nowhere. And all the time on his journey he thought and thought how he could shine brighter than the Bright Bright Stars.

Just as he was about to reach Bethlehem, he had an idea. He came upon one of the Bright Bright Stars just on the outskirts of the small town.

"Good evening, Bright Bright Star," Tink squeaked.

"What are *you* doing here, Tink?" asked the Bright Bright Star.

"I'm on a mission from the Chief Star, and there isn't much time left."

The Bright Bright Star smiled at the idea of the smallest and weakest of the stars carrying out a mission for the Chief.

"What`s the trouble?" the Bright Bright Star said, with a very concerned look on his face.

Tink explained the situation to him and then got very close to him and whispered, "Here's how you can help."

When he heard Tink's plan, the Bright Bright Star smiled. "That's not just bright, Tink. That's *brilliant!*" he said. "But you'll need to go tell the three other Bright Bright Stars in this area also. And you'd better hurry. I can see people are looking for you already!"

"I will! I know we can do it!" Tink said. And he dashed off across the sky as fast as he could move.

He went to each of the other three Bright Bright Stars that the first one had told him about and whispered to them also. One by one, they all twinkled at him and agreed to help.

Once more Tink looked at the directions the Chief Star had given him. Then he raced to take his position high up over the stable in the little town of Bethlehem. From his vantage point way up in the sky, he could see people looking up and wondering where the guiding star was that had been foretold by the prophets. He saw a man and a woman looking very,

very tired as they opened the door to the stable behind the inn. He saw shepherds in the fields watching over their flocks, and, way, way far away he saw three men on camels carrying what looked like precious gifts. All these people, and many, many more than that were counting on him right at this very moment. It was time to carry out his plan.

Very slowly, very carefully, Tink reached into his pocket and took out an object he had carried all the way across the heavens. It was a mirror. He looked up, far, far away into the night sky, up towards the other four Bright Bright Stars and twinkled at them. At this signal they all changed the focus of their star beams and sent them all at once down toward Tink and his mirror. Tink took a deep breath and closed his eyes and glowed and glowed with all his might and then— he *dropped* the mirror!

"Oh *no!*" he cried, as he saw the mirror tumble over and over down and down through the sky. "I'll never be able to lead all these people to the stable now!" Then, as if out of nowhere a voice in his point shouted "BUBBLE GUM!" And Tink took off after the mirror like a shooting star.

As he ran after it, he grabbed a wad of gum and stuffed it into his mouth. Then he reached deep down into his pocket and took out a long kite string he had been carrying around for a long time. When the gum was soft, Tink wrapped it around one end of the string. Then, reaching back with all his Little Star might, he hurled it much much harder and much much faster than he had ever thrown a baseball, so much harder than he had ever thrown a stone—and he aimed it right at the falling mirror.

Then, just before the mirror was about to crash to the ground and splinter into a million pieces, the wad of gum smacked up against it and stuck tight. Tink reeled it in as fast as he could and hurried with all his energy back to the spot high up in the sky above Bethlehem.

The Bright Bright Stars saw what he had done and, to show their appreciation, they beamed their starlight even brighter down to him. Then Tink held the mirror just in the right place to catch all their dazzling beams and, along with his own, flashed them through the skies and above the stable in Bethlehem.

Suddenly the heavens were filled with an incredibly clear and bright light. The tired couple looked up through a stable window. The shepherds awakened from their drowsy sleep in the fields and squinted their eyes. The three men on camels pointed and rode toward it. Then, just as suddenly, the night was christened with the cry of a newborn baby.

Way away, in another corner of the heavens, the Chief Star saw the glow of the light and heard the baby cry. He also through he heard wonderful music and beautiful singing that sounded every bit like the voices of angels he head heard when he was just a Little Star. He smiled to realize that Tink had indeed accomplished his nearly impossible task. And he remembered the passage from Scripture that said "...and a little child shall lead them."

Meanwhile, Tink heard the singing and the baby's cry too. But he was too busy to think. He just held onto that mirror and, with the help of the four other Bright Bright Stars, he beamed and beamed and beamed ever so brightly above that inn and stable in the town of Bethlehem on that first Christmas Day.

So the next time you're out camping with your Papa and you're gazing up in the night sky, see if you can spot Tink. He's a lot older now. Rumor has it that he grew up to be the Chief Star. And although things are a lot different now, he still likes to go out and take his place in the heavens now and then, to shine down on wonderful kids like you.

That's the reason that many people put stars on their Christmas trees—to remember the story of Tink.

Love,

Uncle Chuck

P.S. That is also why you see the very best hotels rating five stars to this very day. And that's where your Uncle Chuck likes to go camping.

HELL

Now that Easter is over and the tomb is empty, there are other things to worry about. Like Hell for instance. I don't know why, but it seems to be the topic of the week. Everybody from patients to my parents to my daughter to an old friend who is getting married has asked me about it, so I am going to bite the bullet and go on the record so I can be properly misquoted in public.

When I explain anything to my daughter Michal, I always start out with the usual world survey of what the possible options are. Next I hone it down to what "a lot of people think." Then, and only then, do I tell her the *Actual Truth*: What I Believe To Be The Case. Michal has gotten pretty used to this and sometimes asks me to skip the first two and go directly to the third to save time. I will do that now.

It is easier to say what Hell is *not* than what it is, at least for openers. And the first thing it is not is a place filled with devils and pitchforks. That image is based largely on the thirteenth century writing of Dante, which has worked its way into popular belief. Besides, that would be too easy and comforting for all of us who think we wouldn't be caught dead there, but relish the possibility of particular others getting their just desserts. In fact, Hell is filled with silence, distance, numbness, equivocation, cold uncertainty, and blinding, hopeless darkness from which there is no return.

Another thing it is not is "down there," unless, of course you are talking about the Australian Outback or Del Rio in the summer. Hell is where you find it. It can be internal, external, a state of mind, a condition, or a feeling. It is less a place than a metaphor, as are all Biblical images. And, like those images, the metaphor powerfully describes the situation.

Dante was correct in describing Hell as a place without hope. (Entering souls read the inscription: "Abandon hope, all who enter here.") There is no hope because Hell is a place with no present. There is only past and future so that we may agonizingly envision how souls came to be there, and contemplate their future in the same place. Spending all our time regretting the past and worrying about the future, we are robbed of the present for eternity.

There is no sense of humor in Hell, not even lawyer jokes. And since justice is God's sense of humor, there is no justice, for there is no presence of God or hope of that presence.

What, then, are the criteria for getting into Hell? There is only one criterion: choosing to go there. And we make that choice with each decision we make every day. Nobody is keeping track of goods and bads we do, sins we commit or omit, guilts or shames or resentments. Nobody except us. And in the end we make a final decision: Where do you want to go? It is God's sense of humor that allows the injustice of those of us who have been less than saintly to ask for, accept and rejoice in forgiveness even at the very last, and thereby choose eternity in God's presence. It is our unremorseful disbelief in God's acceptance and love that inclines us to rebelliously choose Hell.

If all this is true, then why be good? Why not live lives of egocentric, reckless abandon and then cop a plea at the end? One reason is that it would be difficult to do that sincerely and mean it when the time came. And God is no dummy. But the main reason to be good, helpful, sacrificial, honest, healing, respectful, humble and just is that it is in our own best interest. And it is good practice for eternity.

And all this because of one empty tomb.

THINK—TAKE CHANCES

An oxymoron is a combination of words or phrases that contradict each other, such a "giant shrimp," "postal service," "military intelligence," and "congressional ethics."

As I walk out of the parking garage every morning, I have to pass a small sign in the construction area that announces a particular philosophy of life. It reads: "Think. Take no chances." That is an oxymoron.

Now you would think that, as a recent parent of an 8-year-old, I would be propounding this philosophy of life to my daughter at every opportunity—advising her to cautiously approach each situation, anticipate the consequences of her choices, and decide only to take the safest course in order to reach the ripe old age of puberty, and beyond, intact.

Sometimes I do. I tell her, based on a lifetime of experience in such matters, to wear her seat belt, share her Barbies, eat with her mouth closed, pick up her stuff, write thank you notes, and wash her hands after messing with the stupid cats. Such sage wisdom will, undoubtedly, keep her healthy, well thought of, and out of danger. Or so I jokingly try to convince myself.

Because I know, as do we all, that the world is fraught with danger at every turn. Control is an illusion. Good is not always rewarded, nor is evil always punished. So why do we tell our kids otherwise? Perhaps it is to shield them from finding out too soon that the world is not as neatly ordered as we present it. So we tell them to think, be careful, close cover before striking, look both ways, and always ask yourself "What would my Daddy do if he knew about this?"

The truth is that most of us were brought up with the admonition from our own parents to "Think. Take no chances." But the truth is also that few of us ever got anywhere by doing so. Recall, for a moment, the choice points in your life, the forks in the road, the chances you took, the risky endeavors upon which you embarked without knowing beforehand (and often without thinking beforehand) where they would end.

For most of us, if we had really thought about all the possible consequences or ramifications of our decision, we would have safely stayed put and not budged from the couch. But, fortunately, we ignored the advice of our parents and took a chance: moved, bought a house, fell in love, changed jobs, dropped everything and traveled, had a child, broke up a relationship, bought something we wanted, volunteered to help someone, sacrificed time, money or talent for someone else, let someone help us, healed a hurt.

And regardless of how they came out, the decisions based on risk paid off, because, as the ad for

Jamaica used to say "If you never go, you'll never know." Likewise, the existential truism on every soft drink bottle: "No Deposit. No Return."

Now this is not to suggest that we foolishly barge into dangerous or risky circumstances without somehow considering the cost, thinking about what may or may not happen; but it is to suggest that perhaps we present two messages to our children and loved ones, even to ourselves. Intellectually, what comes out of our mouths is the construction sign that we wish we could put in the room of every kid, especially adolescent, we know: "Think. Take no chances." Behaviorally, what we model with our lives, is usually the opposite. And our kids, being the perceptive people that they are, pick up both, and do what we do, not what we say, just as we did with our parents. And that is a very good thing.

In the same way, God takes chances on us, forgiving, believing, healing, suffering with us, agonizing over us, laughing at us and, hopefully, with us. So to follow God is to live in a world with oxymora, at least of the kind on the construction sign. It is to live in a world where we question and move forward; where we ask and change; where we live by the model God has set out for us: "Think. And take chances." Because, as all of us know well, there will come a time when there are no more chances to take.

SUGAR I — The Rescue

The cat's name is Sugar. A more inappropriate name I have never known—unless the sugar on your table is a dirty grey with whiskers protruding ominously from the bowl and claws ready to grab you.

Sugar and I have, after eight months of my being in his territory (by marriage), come to an agreement. We terrorize each other. He knows I hate his being in the house—shedding his fur globs on my computer, drooling on my pillow, spraying only *my* things in the closet. So he patrols the perimeter of the house like a cat-burglar, seeking entry at every turn. If Michal opens the door to the garage, the back patio or the living room, Sugar is there, ready to pounce through the opening. Every morning when I leave for work Sugar sits on the doormat, smirking, knowing that I know he will leap inside when I'm gone and hide in unknown places until he can go mess with my stuff.

I, on the other hand, race into the driveway (his favorite sleeping spot) each afternoon at 90 mph, and come to a screeching halt right at his nose. When I catch him in the house with my stuff, I eject him with form that would be the envy of an Olympic javelin thrower. (I like to think of him as The Grey Projectile). When he sits on the porch railing, I poke at him until he 'jumps' off, sometimes holding on with his front claws awhile to attempt some chinning.

He only uses the garage litter box when my car is parked there. I only water the lawn when he's sleeping under the bushes. He only claws at the screen when I am napping. I only put out the cat food when he's not around (so the other, old, decrepit, blind, senile, drooly cat can eat it all. I like him.)

When Michal went to camp in July, Sugar vanished after the second day. I noticed because the target was no longer in the driveway. I supposed he sensed he had lost his primary protector and knew we were down to "no holds barred." So I forgot about him and gave the other old, decrepit cat double portions. I hoped Sugar would return in about twenty years, by which time we probably would have sold the house.

Michal came home a week later, and we made our usual walk to the mailbox. On the way back we simultaneously heard a familiar sound. A wretched meow emanated from the neighbor's garage. I ignored it. Michal yanked my hand. We checked and there was Sugar, meowing what little brains he has out. And the neighbor had moved a month ago for parts unknown. Apparently an agent opened the house to show it and the cat ran for the garage and got locked in. Michal and Debi got hysterical when I inadvertently used the phrase "starving to death." They also did not appreciate my calmly waving at him through the dirty window with a smile.

To make a long story short (film at 11), I tried (not *too* hard) to break into the house. I called the Police, Fire and Sheriff, all of whom couldn't help and politely suggested that I call the other one. They also asked if I was *certain* no one was in the house and obliquely implied (not for recording) that I might "assist" one of the doors or windows to open. Debi finally (with divine intervention—she's the one with connections) located the owner. He opened the garage and handed me the skinny, hacked-off cat. Having me there to rescue him was the ultimate humiliation for Sugar, I am sure. I even let him in the living room for a while to be with Michal.

Sometimes our relationship with God is like that. We bug each other at every turn. God tries to get in; we keep God out. God gets into our stuff; we get angry. And vice versa. We challenge God (often at the equivalent of 90 mph); God smirks back. We infuriate God; God infuriates us. We each do our best to keep the other off balance, clawing at the screen or bumping the porch railing.

But then one of us gets locked in the garage, accidentally or by our own effort. At the hospital God is presented to us through people who are locked in the garage of sickness, despair and death. Elsewhere people get locked into poverty, homelessness, psychological dysfunction, or job burnout. We do what we can to help them out of that garage, and thereby get God out as well. And God does the same for us when we call for help from our own garages, which, once we are out, become empty tombs.

When I left for work this morning Sugar was on the doormat. And I'm sure he'll be waiting for me tonight, smirk intact.

GOD'S LAUGHTER

Werewolves. We have graduated from cats to werewolves.

At two o'clock in the morning (after Sugar the cat finally stopped harassing me and quit clawing at the screen) I was awakened by the unmistakable sound of muffled sniffles beside the bed. I opened one eye, hoping Debi would hear her first. She didn't, or pretended she didn't, so this one was mine.

"What's the matter?" I mumbled, trying to sound interested and in control, but with the tone of voice that says "give me the short version."

"N..n..nothing," Michal replied, mopping up her spurting tears with her old, beat up bunnies that have nearly disintegrated from such soakings.

"Then let's go back to bed!" I said, rolling out and walking her back down the hallway. As we entered her room I stepped carefully, remembering previous impalements from assorted Barbie accessories. "Are you sure you don't want to tell me what happened?"

"N..no.." she said tentatively.

I always take my daughter at her word, especially at such an hour, so I tucked her in, kissed her good night and groped my way back down the hall.

Ten minutes later the muffled sniffles returned.

"What's the matter?"

"B..bad dream."

We walked back down the hall, turned on her bedside light and sat on her bed. "You wanna tell me about the dream?"

Silence. I knew it was serious.

"Michal, I can't help if I don't know what the problem is. Tell me the dream."

She peeked out from between two ragged bunny ears and tentatively whispered: "Werewolves."

"Werewolves?" I asked. "You dreamed about werewolves? Where did you hear about werewolves?"

"Amy."

I made a mental note to personally scare the bejeebers out of Amy at the next sleepover. "Ooooohhh, Michal," I said reassuringly. "Kids do that all the time to other kids just to scare them." I then let out the words I swore I would never, ever, ever speak.."Why I remember when I was your age, we were camping out one night during a full moon and we got this other kid to believing in werewolves.."

Michal's eyes got bigger and bigger with the story. Nobody told me that one of the rules is: The more you say a word the more vivid it becomes in a kid's mind. So after the 45th use of the word "Werewolf," Michal was cringing under the blanket, covered with increasing numbers of stuffed animals. Finally, she squeaked out: "Daddy?"

"What?"

She emerged from the cavern of animals and sheets. "Well, when this happens with Mom, she usually tells me a funny story and I get my mind off the dream and go back to sleep."

"Oooohhh. A funny story!" (Why don't they hand out manuals with 8 year olds?) "Sure, I can handle that."

"It was a pretty bad dream. I think I need *two* funny stories."

Michal snuggled down amidst the sea of stuffing and endured two funny stories from Dad, one of which she laughed at. The first one. The second one she asked me why it was funny. "Oh, yeah," she said, yawning. Then she grinned that Dad-tolerating grin of hers and went to sleep.

As I tiptoed back down the hallway, I realized she had taught me yet another theological lesson. The way to approach evil is not by rational explanation, or bolstering one's defenses, or even by much prayer and fasting. The way to deal with evil is the same way God deals with it—by laughter.

When some tragedy strikes (disease, airplanes, accidents, hostages, politicians, etc.) it is only a matter of time before the jokes begin. When Halloween arrives— the night of All Hallow's Eve, when the spirits of the dead are said to have free reign—we dress up like them, make parodies of their tales, and wear costumes through the streets of the neighborhood, even their graveyards.

God, too, laughs at evil. It is so ludicrous to God, so silly, so incongruous with the way things are, so out of place with God's mercy and forgiveness and love, that it can only be met, ultimately, and defused, permanently, with laughter. It is God's laughter that redeems unredeemable situations, that heals unhealable hurts, that loves the unlovable in us all.

Thank you Michal for the information on how to handle werewolves. And for the Barbie spike heel in my foot.

REVELATION

It is the season of Thanksgiving and I am giving thanks because I had a revelation in church last Sunday. Now, that is a very odd place for me to have such a thing, since I am not a fancier of organized religious services and find them generally boring, overly long, musically distracting and monotonously read. The reason I go is the subject for another column. Suffice it to say that during one of the few unboring parts we were reading Psalm 121 about lifting our eyes up to the hills from whence cometh our help and I got to thinking about the earthquake in San Francisco where the hills were alive with everything but music. I wondered if the people thought there really wasn't much help to be had there.

I had heard some of the usual "God spared this person because..." nonsense on the news earlier in the week and wondered what exactly people thought God should do in an earthquake:

a. Stop the earthquake from happening in the first place.

b. Miraculously intervene and prevent anyone from being harmed.

c. Capriciously intervene and prevent only those people who God thinks deserve it from being harmed.

d. Intervene so that only people who have not yet accomplished their purpose are spared, thus reinforcing the Divine Plan Model For Disaster Management.

e. Use the event to do away with a bunch of bad people (ala Sodom & Gomorrah).

f. All of the above.

g. Other.

My own answer is, of course, "g" because I believe that God cannot do "a" through "f." God cannot miraculously or capriciously intervene or interfere and still keep the contract that we are free to decide and nature is free to erupt, blow, flood, quake and devastate us with diseases over which we have little control. (For a more detailed discussion of this theology, see the book *Surviving Death*.)

But then comes along Psalm 121 Sunday morning saying that "the Lord is your shade on your right hand. The sun shall not smite you by day, nor the moon by night." And furthermore... "The Lord will keep you from all evil; he will keep your life."

At first appearance these concepts made no sense together. But that's where the revelation comes in, because at that very moment it occurred to me what the fallacy is, and I hear it at the bedside of dying patients all the time.

The error is that we take passages like Psalm 121 to mean that God will protect us from death, because that is what we fear most. But passage after passage indicates that God will protect us, watch over us, be with us, keep us close, whether we are alive *or* dead. In Psalm 121 we are assured that God will protect our life no matter what form it takes, physical or otherwise. It is almost as if God has not even considered death as something from which we *need* protection; it is too inconsequential in the Big Picture. There are, in fact, many more things from which we need protection than death, many things worse than death's finality, many things more horrid than death's pallor, many things more painful than death's end.

What, you might reasonably ask, has all this to do with Thanksgiving? The answer is "everything." For when we give thanks on this occasion, it is important to remember what we are giving thanks for. Is it for the good things that have happened, the successes, the completions, the new possessions? Or is it for the overwhelming sense of the promise that, regardless of the "changes and chances of this world," our life is kept by One who transcends death and offers hope in its place.

As a brain cancer patient once told me, "It's okay with me if I live and it's okay with me if I die. Because either place I'm loved." For that and for other revelations we may be truly thankful.

JOSEPH

I am writing this on the afternoon of Christmas Eve as my wife does last minute arranging and my daughter sits reading Christmas books to get even more in the spirit, if that is possible. Our hot water just came back on and it looks as though the wintry blast is finally loosening its grip on us. At work we have attended an overwhelming number of deaths this past week, deaths of persons from 32 to 85, including two old friends. As the funeral service reminds us: "In the midst of life we are in death. In the midst of death, life." Christmas is upon us and it is hard to be joyous.

Surprisingly enough, the person I'm thinking most about tonight is Joseph. We don't hear much about him. He's sort of a spectator on the Divine Stage of events. He unobtrusively fades into the background while everyone else takes center stage. Everything had seemed to be going fairly well. He was an accomplished carpenter with a good business. He had found a woman with whose family the proper pre-arrangements had been made, and he was happily betrothed to Mary. Then the unforeseeable, the unwanted, the improbable occurred. And suddenly he was angry. He felt thrown off balance. This could not happen to him.

His sense of what was right and proper and fair was offended. It was terrible timing, even embarrassing timing, on God's part.

And yet, because he was "a just man" he determined to do the right thing and quietly divorce her. But that very night an angel appeared to Joseph in a dream, as angels are wont to do, and gave Joseph some more data. "There is more to this than meets the eye," said the angel. "God is up to something here that transcends you, Mary, the baby and even me."

"Like what?" said the embittered Joseph.

"Like hope..." replied the patient angel. "...And mercy, and forgiveness, and rebirth, and even love."

So Joseph took a deep breath and made his decision. Reluctantly, he chose trust. And the payoff was of eternal proportions.

And we are exactly like him. Like Joseph, we seldom occupy center stage; we unobtrusively fade into the background of work or family, or ultimately of history as other events go on with or without us. From time to time our lives seem to be fairly in order, or we are in love, or we have accomplished a goal, or seem to be on a plateau, or stop for a moment to take a breather. Then the unforeseeable, the unwanted, the improbable occurs. Someone we know dies. And suddenly we are angry. We feel thrown off balance. How could this happen? Our sense of what is right and proper and fair is offended. It is terrible timing, even embarrassing timing, on God's part, on the person's part, on our part.

But because God does not want us to be despairing, God reaches out to us in some angel-equivalent way, through words or feelings or physical embraces, and affirms that there is more to this than meets the eye; that something is going on here that transcends you, me, old friends and anyone else who comes to mind, living or dead.

"Like what?" our embittered minds reply.

"Like hope..." replies the messenger, "...and mercy, and forgiveness, and rebirth, and even love."

So, like Joseph, we take a deep breath and make our decision. Reluctantly, hopefully, we choose to risk again. And the payoff for us has eternal dimensions.

The night of death is the eve of rebirth.

"The light shines in the darkness, and the darkness has not overcome it."

I was going through my next year's pocket calendar today, busily filling in all the weekly meetings and appointments and obligations that are already scheduled for me. I stopped for a moment when I realized how comforting this seemed, filling in all that blank space and getting control of unknown times and dates. I considered all the events of the past week, the deaths of friends and the young woman and the old man; the light of Christmas breaking into the despair of all this death; and the image of Joseph came clear in my mind. I put the calendar down and went to sing carols.

In the midst of life we are in death. In the midst of death, life.

AN ANGEL NAMED BUBBA

(Nathan Brown Joslin is a four-year-old friend of mine.)

Dear Nathan:

What a difference a year makes. Last Christmas you were a shy three-year-old and your house was filled with Nathan things. This year you are an outgoing four, helping to look after toys that belong to the lovely little Lillian Ross. You really are very good with her, Nathan, even if she is hard to keep track of sometimes.

But some things never change, and here I am, the Family Theologian, still explaining Christmas. The story, this time, is about a shepherd boy named Aaron, and, of all things, his little sister, Karin.

Very late, one cold night on a hillside overlooking the quiet little town of Bethlehem, Aaron tossed another twig onto the burning campfire. He was bit older than you, Nate, about your friend Sam's age, and he was worried.

His Mama and Papa were in the next village helping a sick relative. They would be gone all night. There was no one else to watch the flock of sheep but him. And he was all alone.

Well, not quite *all* alone. There were the twenty-five sheep. And the dog who sat, with its head on its paws, watching for any movements or sounds. And then—he glanced to the side of the campfire—there was Karin.

Karin was three years old, and into everything—except sitting still. She needed a separate sheep dog for herself, Aaron thought, as he sighed a deep sigh and wondered how he would make it through the night. Her big dark eyes looked over at him, and the moon shone down on her long black hair.

"Okay, okay. You're cute and we both know it." He walked over and saw down beside her on the blanket in front of the fire. "But we have to stay very close together tonight, Karin. We have to watch these sheep and not let any get away, or..." he said, looking out over the hillside, "...not let any be eaten by wolves.."

"WOLVES!?"

"Yes, Karin! Wolves!" That got her attention, he thought. "Huge, vicious animals with teeth like this...." He opened his mouth wide and bared his teeth and growled. The dog raised its head inquisitively. Karin bit her quivering lip and seemed about to cry.

"But don't you worry, little sister," he said, putting his arm around her and smiling. "As long as you stick next to me everything will be fine."

"I'll...I'll be right...*here!*" She snuggled closer to her older brother. "Just don't leave me alo..."

At that moment the dog stood up but kept perfectly still.

"What is it, boy?" Aaron asked. He knew the well-trained sheep dog had detected some movement in the flock. "What do you hear?"

Just then the sheep broke out in a noisy bleating, and the dog ran off to the far side of the flock.

"What is it?" Karin asked.

"Could be a wolf, or it could just be they got spooked by their own shadows. Sheep are pretty dumb, you know." He stood and glanced in the direction of the noise. "I'd better go check." He pointed to the fire. "You stay here and keep the fire going."

"But what if...?"

"Just don't run off, Karin. You got that?"

"Uh-huh," she said, unconvincingly.

"I'll be right back," her brother said, and he disappeared into the darkness.

Karin sat looking back and forth with her eyes but not moving her head. She didn't like being left behind again. She was big enough to help. And she wasn't afraid of any old wolves, either.

The fire popped and she jumped to her feet. Well, not *too* afraid, anyway.

Just then she heard a strange flapping noise behind her. Her little heart nearly beat through her chest. She was afraid to turn around and afraid not to. When the flapping stopped, she slowly turned and looked up, not believing her wide open eyes.

There in front of her stood a six foot creature with

wings and a scowl on its face.

"Where are your parents, kid?" the thing said.

"Whaaaa...What...did...did you...say...?"

"Are you deaf, child? I said: 'Where are your parents?' Your folks. Big People. You savvy?"

"They're not...here." She started trembling and the edges of her little mouth started to pull down. "What...*are*...you?"

"Oh, good grief. Don't go cryin' on me, darlin'. I cain't take a female in tears." The huge creature walked over and knelt down next to her. "I'm an angel, kid. You heard of angels, haven't ya?"

"Well, yes. I think so." She pointed to his back. "Are those...wings?"

"I'm afraid so." The angel looked around, then back at the wide-eyed child. "Now, lissen here, kid. I was supposed to meet your parents at this spot and give them some news..."

"What's...your...name?"

The angel looked at her with a smirk. He held out his weathered hand. "Bubba," he said. "What's yours?"

She put her tiny hand in his. "Karin," she said. "Bubba's a funny name. Where did you come from? Heaven?"

"Close, child. Texas. It hasn't been invented yet, but..."

"And what are those?" She pointed to his feet.

"Tony Lama Bullhides, darlin'. You cain't get 'em in Jerusalem."

"No. I mean those." She pointed to his heels."

"Spurs. But I didn't come here for no fashion show. I'm supposed to tell your folks that...wait a minute here..." Bubba fumbled inside his white jump suit and took out a slip of paper. "Here it is..." He cleared his throat. "Be not afraid." He looked at her. "I guess we already covered that, didn't we?" She smiled at him. "Okay, uh...Behold! I bring you good news of a great joy which will come to all the people; for to you is born this day in the City of David a saviour, who is Christ the Lord. And this will be a sign for you; you will find a babe wrapped in swaddling cloths and lying in a manger. And the baby's name is Jesus."

"You did that real good," she said, smiling up at him.

"Thanks. Some ol' boy name of Luke's gonna write it all down later."

"I can't read yet. But my brother's trying to teach me. He..."

"Yore brother? Where's *he* at?" Bubba scowled.

"He's checking on the sheep..."

"Well, let me go git him and then I can read this to him and git on my rounds."

Bubba stood and slowly rose from the ground into the air.

"I see him. You stay here, Karin. We'll be right back."

No sooner had Bubba disappeared from sight than Karin started thinking.

"Bethlehem isn't far off," she thought. "I wonder if I could find that Saviour-baby Jesus. I'd sure like to take him something for his birthday." She felt the rough blanket around her shoulders. "Maybe it could use this blanket to keep warm tonight!"

Karin carefully arranged some stones in front of the fire. Then she ran into the night in the direction of Bethlehem.

The dog barked menacingly at Bubba's descending Tony Lama's.

"Git holt of that critter, boy!" he hollered at the frozen Aaron.

Aaron stood stark still watching the huge creature come down through the air. He didn't know whether to run or attack. Fortunately, his wobbly legs would do neither. But he did call off the dog.

"Here, boy." The dog came to him and Aaron held it by the collar. "But if you give me any trouble, mister, I let the dog go. And he's a killer."

Bubba looked up to the sky and muttered, "Kids and dogs. I cain't believe the Boss *did* this to me..." He eyed the boy warily. "Hang on to that mutt, kid, and lissen up. I need to make this fast. Name's Bubba. I hail from Texas. These here are boots and spurs. Forget about tryin' to understand that. Just lissen to the message. `Unto you is born....'"

"You're a little late, mister. I already know *that*."

"What? How could you...?"

"I just helped that sheep over there give birth to that baby lamb."

Bubba looked at the tiny lamb bleating in the darkness.

That's right cute, son. But it ain't what I had in mind, exactly. As I was tellin' yore sister..."

"Omigawsh," Aaron said. "I nearly forgot about her. I'd better get back to the campfire before she..."

"Just a second boy. Let me check." Bubba rose high in the ski, then drifted back down. "We're in trouble, kid. She's gone. But she did leave a bunch of stones in the shape of an arrow—and it pointed toward Bethlehem."

Aaron sat down on a rock with his head in his hands. The dog, understanding, licked his face. "They'll kill me. My parents will kill me."

Bubba looked at the dejected child. "And the Boss'll banish me to Cleveland if I don't get all my announcin' done. But what the heck. Okay, son. Tell that dog there to watch the sheeps." He reached out his huge hand. "Then climb aboard and we'll see can we find her."

Seconds later Bubba and Aaron were flying through the air. The night landscape was lighted by a giant silver moon and a huge shining star that seemed to hang in the sky over a certain part of the town.

"That's the biggest star I ever saw!" Aaron said, pointing above them.

"And the biggest one you ever *will* see, son," Bubba replied. "It's the one that stands over the stable where the Saviour-baby Jesus is sleepin'."

"That's IT, Bubba! Go down there! That's where Karin is! I just *know* it!"

"Well, okay. If you say so. But I'd check out the circus first..."

The two slowly moved over Bethlehem and hovered over the stable.

"I don't see her, boy."

"Let's go down and look inside. I still bet she's in there!" Aaron said, as they softly landed outside the stable door and carefully opened it.

The huge angel and the little boy walked hand in hand toward the farthest stall, where animals were gathered around the young couple trying to keep warm in the hay. There, snuggled against a donkey, was Karin, half asleep. Her droopy eyes were glued to the little baby wrapped in her own woolen blanket.

Aaron sat beside her, put his arm around her, and looked and looked.

"He didn't have any blanket," Karin said, "...so I gave him mine."

"That was a right nice thing to do, little lady," Bubba said. "But we've got to get you home now. Your parents will be looking for you..."

"Oh, no, Bubba," Aaron said. "They're not coming back till..."

"Trust me, boy. They'll be home tonight."

Karin looked at him. "But how do you know...?"

"I'm an *angel*, remember! It's my *job* to know." He picked them both up in his arms, winked at the couple and the baby in the manger, and floated out through an open loft at the top of the barn.

As they flew across the sky with the moon at their back, Aaron asked: "Just what is a Saviour-baby, Bubba?"

Bubba hesitated a second and said: "It's a baby who grow up to love us more than we do ourselves, forgive us more than we do ourselves, want more for us than we want for ourselves." He looked down at the nodding Karin. "It's a baby who grows up to accept our strength and to know our weaknesses; a baby who grows up to be an adult who loves enough to die to change the world through us, if we'll let him."

Aaron looked back at the stable in the distance. "Gee, I'd like to help him."

"That's all he asks, son, is to give it yore best shot." Bubba hugged the two children. "And to love one another."

A silence came over them as they slowly descended by the campfire. Karin woke up in time to say goodbye to Bubba as he floated up out of sight.

"Now y'all be good, and remember to tell your parents what I told you!" He looked over the hill. "They'll be here in a few minutes."

The brother and sister waved until they could see him no more. Just then, their Mama and Papa came into sight, carrying the baby lamb that Aaron had helped with earlier.

"Mama! Papa!" the two yelled. "We saw an angel and went to Bethlehem, and Karin gave the Saviour-baby Jesus her wool blanket...and..."

Their stunned parents sat them down with the lamb by the fire and listened patiently as the excited children told their story. They hugged them close and uttered a prayer for their safety, no matter what had really happened. Then they put down some soft blankets and covered Aaron and Karin up to go to sleep.

Aaron, struggling against drowsiness, poked his sister lying next to him. "What will we call the new lamb, Karin?"

A long pause followed. Then her soft, sleepy voice whispered: "Texas."

Their father, overhearing their talk, asked: "What's a 'Texas'?"

A small speck passed in front of the great star in the heavens, as Karin replied: "It hasn't...been invented...yet." And the children were sure they heard the flapping of wings far away.

And that is why the angel on top of your Uncle Chuck's tree has little tiny boots on it, to remind us all of the wonderful news of Jesus' birth, as told to the shepherds by Bubba in Bethlehem.

Love,

Uncle Chuck

GOING HOME

Michal was upset the other day and wishing we could move back to the old house on Jubilee Trail, where she knew the kids, and the school, and the neighborhood, and the house wasn't so scary and different. In times of stress or sadness or frustration she wants to go back to the familiar.

And I do the same thing. During a particularly busy and stressful weekend of being on call I have been listening the whole time to an Oldies station and playing old songs on the piano, finding much comfort and happy memories in them both, so I understand Michal's desire to go backwards in time.

The Israelites wanted to do the same thing when Moses led them out into the wilderness; even slavery looked better than what he had taken them into, and nostalgia obscured the whips on their backs and the forced labor in favor of memories of a roof over their heads and certainty in daily life.

So I got to wondering: What is so attractive about the past? Is it that we think we mastered it and derive comfort from that fact? Is it that it is known rather than unknown and therefore safe or in control? Is it that it is over with and we survived it and can talk about it (and embellish it)? Is it that, compared to an uncertain, unknown today and tomorrow, yesterday seems tamed, manageable, certain?

I wonder how I can tell Michal the awful truth that we all have learned through painful attempt after painful attempt—that you can't go home again. Things change. People are different. The house you grew up in looks suddenly smaller. Perspective is convoluted in our minds, and seduces us into trying to go back, only to disappoint us when we get there.

I may take her back to the old house and watch what happens, watch her shattered expectations fall down around her, and be there to hug her and help clean up the mess when it doesn't quite work the way she thought it would.

As painful as the truth is, the only way out is forward, into the unknown. It is important to reminisce, to remember past successes and failures and even to wax nostalgic about some things that we know look a lot better in hindsight than they did at the time (largely because of present embellishments.) But it is also important not to live in the past, ignoring the present and robbing ourselves of the pleasures, dangers and accomplishments of the future.

Such a stance is, of course, a risky one. Thanks be to God that we do not venture there alone.

EDEN

Last Sunday in church they read the stories of the Garden of Eden and the Temptation of Jesus by the devil in the wilderness. The interesting thing about both stories is that the problems begin just when everything is going great. It is right after everything is pleasant and good and everybody is naked and nobody is ashamed that the serpent appears with his questions and his certainty. And it is right after Jesus is baptized by John and at his spiritual apogee that he meets up with the devilish temptations of arrogance, self-interest and power.

It is, of course, possible to draw several conclusions from this. One would be that it is just when we think we are on good terms with God that we are at our weakest spiritually and most vulnerable to the temptation of certainty. Another is that the devil likes to come around and mess things up just when life is at its best. The job promotion comes through and suddenly it's time for orthodontia. You just get your management team in place and someone gets promoted or someone else resigns to work for your competitor. The house gets picked up and clean and the cat prances through the cat door with mud on its furry paws. The car gets paid off—and falls apart.

Perhaps the lesson here is that the biggest mistake (sin?) is that of *stability*. It is as though we are being told that our lives are not to be rigidly fixed, that too much stability results in stagnation, moral and spiritual arrogance, a rigid calcification of our ways, and an inflexible view of the universe, God and ourselves.

So what would it mean, I wonder, if the snake and the devil are, in fact, tools of God to keep us growing, changing, developing our understanding of ourselves, each other and our God? Perhaps the things we see as evil are not tests or obstacles but normal events in our lives that keep us focused on the present rather than the past, that refuse to let us become inert and unyielding in our thoughts, and that draw us into change and newness.

In any case, whether we resist the temptations before us or eat the apples, we are changed by the experience, and we can never not know what we know now. The important point is to continue our journey forward together, serving one another, serving God in the process, as we smile at the snake, grin at the devil, and write the check for the orthodontist.

THE PLANET OF MISTAKES

Meagen (age 6) just spilled her orange juice in the back yard—for the third time. Bobbie (8) got more of her taco on the kitchen floor than in the taco. And Michal (also 8) is sweeping up the cat food that magically ended up on the garage floor instead of the feeding bowls. Of course, nothing was their fault. I didn't put the lid on the crayon mug tight enough, Debi had the cheese grated too thin, and the cat tripped Michal (on purpose).

One of the worst things about being a kid is that you remind your parents and any other adult who has the misfortune of being around when you make a mistake, of what they were like then they were your age. Or maybe worse than that is when adults realize that we continue doing the same thing even now. When we spill the juice, drop the taco, or dump the cat food, why is it that our first thought is, "How can I get out of this?" When we make a mistake at work, say something improper to someone or forget something we said we would do, what is so hard about saying "Oops, sorry about that." "I apologize." "I regret doing that." "I won't do it again."

Somewhere we must have learned we are supposed to be perfect, or received harsh penalties (real or imagined) for not being perfect. We even are told that scripture says "You must be perfect as your Heavenly Father is perfect." So we go through our lives acting as though our Heavenly Father, or Supervisor, or Parent In Our Head, or Somebody is going to zap us big time if we mess up.

But the Greek word "perfect" in Scripture means "whole" or "mature." And to be whole means making mistakes—and apologizing; being hurt or wronged—and forgiving; accepting our *im*perfection as our normal state and, at least as importantly, as the normal state of others, and going on.

Lent is a good time to reflect on our imperfection, to realize that it is important to do the best job we can do, personally and professionally, at home with family and at work with patients, families and each other. It is *not* okay to do sloppy or incomplete or insensitive work, but it is okay in the pursuit of doing good work to make mistakes, to accept the responsibility for them, and to continue doing our best on the way to fuller maturity and wholeness. The theme of Lent is not only repentance, but forgiveness.

Michal, after the umpteenth error learning to type said, "I think we should call this place 'The Planet of Mistakes.'" And it is. Thank God it is also the planet of imperfection and mercy.

A LETTER TO NIKKY

(Adele Lorusso was Director of Social Services for St. David's Hospital. She died at 38 of cancer. Her two-old-son, Nikky, played in the grass by the podium as the letter was read.)

Dear Nikky:

It is a sad day. Your mother, Adele, has died, and all of us here are gathered to mourn her death in our own way. We mourn the loss of how we knew her: wife, daughter, relative, colleague, and for most of us here, friend, because we were lucky enough to be counted by her as one of those. So, intermingled in our mourning is the bittersweet celebration of her life and of the fun and joy she brought to our lives with her.

Early on, in January, when your mother was initially diagnosed with the cancer, she asked me if I would conduct her funeral when the time came. She and I were practical about such matters because we worked together for many years on the cancer unit at St. David's and had gone through many deaths together. But let me assure you that she was in no hurry to have me do this. She did everything she possibly could to stay alive for you, for your dad, for herself, and for us all.

She also asked me if I would keep in touch with you from time to time, and tell you about her, so you would be reminded about who she was. I will combine those two duties now.

Let me tell you, first of all, that Adele loved and cared deeply. She loved your daddy, her parents, and treated her friends like family. She cared about stray cats and stray people. She would do anything she could to help others, whether she was involved with them personally as friends or professionally as clients.

She was a good friend in a world where good friends are scarce: friends you can count on, trust, know will be there in the bad times when you need them and the good times to play with and celebrate with when you want them.

And that is how I will remember Adele. She was funny, Nikky, really funny. She had a wonderful laugh that made you laugh with her; she could tell great jokes, appreciate other people's funny stories, and couldn't wait to up the ante with one on herself. Even in the hospital in the midst of her illness, she wore funny pins and T-shirts that your daddy brought her.

She loved to socialize. There was no such thing as a five-minute conversation with Adele. Whether discussing clients, or sharing stories, or planning the next party to spend the Hospice on-call money we had earned as a team, Adele lived to talk and listen—which is why she was so competent in her job.

And she worked hard, too. She put in long hours, took work home, got jobs done ahead of time, even came in once a week during her chemotherapy as long as she could to, as she put it, "take care of details." For that reason, we all relied on her, trusted her competence and reliability, knew that when she spoke for an issue or a person, we had better listen to her point of view.

Because as much as your mother loved, Nikky, she also hated. She hated injustice, prejudice, unfairness, inequality, disadvantage. One time she even quit a job over those issues, and later received a letter inviting her back to work and acknowledging that she had been right. She hated the unfairness of her illness. And it was unfair, unjust, uncalled for, unreasonable. It was not planned or deserved, willed or conjured, the product of wrong thoughts or actions. Her illness was aggressive, devastating, producing no good news for her to hear. And still, even in the midst of her anger, Adele maintained her own sense of fairness. She was a fair woman, Nikky, and that is unusual in a selfish and unfair world.

And, with that same fairness, she would acknowledge that she was not a saint. She had her faults, just as I do, and you do, and all of the people at this service do. The difference with Adele was that she knew it better than anyone else and spent a lot of her time worrying that some base was left uncovered somewhere, and she'd be caught being responsible for not covering it. She worried enough for both of us—which probably kept us out of a lot of trouble, actually, but took up a lot of time that might have been spent on more fun activities, like another party.

Though she would be shocked to hear me say it, she was a religious woman, though not in the traditional sense. She had a spirituality that led her to embrace strong moral and ethical standards.

One of the best things about your mother, Nikky, was that she was unabashedly insatiable. She could never get enough of time with people. She wanted to be in on everything, never miss a chance to go out to eat nachos and drink a beer with people she liked. I remember after one particularly horrible day of being poked and probed and radiated and physically and emotionally turned every which way but loose, Adele was being wheeled out of radiology looking drained and exhausted. A number of her friends were in the waiting room, and Adele overheard someone suggest going out for a beer and Mexican food. They were all overwhelmed to hear this weakened voice from the wheelchair in the doorway whisper "Let's go." And they did.

Finally, Nikky, there were some things she wanted me to pass along to you and to all those gathered today. The first thing she said was, "Tell them to appreciate who and what they've got now. Don't take anything or anyone for granted." And those words were not just from her sudden illness, Nikky. They were learned at the bedside of dying patients and families over years, learned, as most of us at the hospital learn them, by being deeply involved with many of those for whom we have cared. They are good words, wise words, powerful words. Heed them and you will live well and play well, regardless of the length of your years.

The second thing she wanted to tell you was to be committed to something beyond yourself that would make a difference, that would leave the world a better place than it was before you were here. Your mother was a good example of that, Nikky. She left not only the world and all the people she helped, but my life, our lives, better than they were before we knew her. These are gentle words, kind words, giving words. Heed them and you will give well and be well-supported by giving people.

Lastly, she wanted desperately for you to know how much she loved you, wanted you to know and love her, wanted to be there for your second birthday in June, and your third and your thirteenth and your thirtieth. And she wanted you to be a playful, loving person to both give love and be able to accept love. Heed these words and you will mature well and love well.

So that is it for now, Nikky. There will be more to come, from your daddy and grandparents, from many of us here, from other friends and relatives, from myself—from your mother through all of us.

We are grateful for the gift that Adele was to us in this place and time, and we trust and pray that she continues on her journey in peace and comfort. May we also remember her words to you, Nikky, about living here and now, giving beyond ourselves, and loving into deep attachments.

As your mother knew well, and told us repeatedly, life is too short to do anything else.

Sincerely,

Chuck Meyer

CONCEPTION

I was wadding up some newspaper for the last fireplace of Spring when I found it. The headline, like a slamming door, startled me to attention. I unwadded the paper and sat back to read that the Laredo City Council had passed a resolution declaring that "life begins at conception." So...we can all sleep well tonight knowing that that issue has been decisively concluded—and by such a knowledgeable, erstwhile body. Perhaps next week they could take up the question of life on other planets.

It seems to me that the larger concern here is one of the search for certainty, for stability, for a firm system of belief or code of behavior that will stand, unfaltering against the test of time. For the same reason some state legislatures passed severe restrictions on not only the practice of abortion but also the mere provision of information about it. But the activists of the 60's quickly learned that you cannot legislate morality; and the seekers of certainty must today learn that you cannot legislate scientific opinion.

What these events indicate is the lack of consensus on what is "right," "good," "proper," "appropriate," or "moral." All around us the bastions of certainty are falling; things we have taken for granted for decades are now no longer true. Not long ago we would have still believed in the "anti-American communist conspiracy" that kept Eastern Europe in deadlock and Berlin divided by a heinous, ugly wall. Today, the Wall is gone, Germany is reunited, Mandala is free in South Africa, the Soviet Union has dissolved, Eastern Europe is in the throes of independence, Nicaragua has elected a woman president, and Terry Waite and all the other hostages have been released.

In another field, all previous assumptions about the provision of healthcare in the United States are being challenged. New questions are being asked: Is healthcare a right or a privilege? Should a certain amount be mandatory (universal access)? Should there be limits on the amount of care offered and given? Who should receive expensive, extraordinary care? How should we pay for it? In five years the entire system will be radically changed as these questions are answered.

Basic structures all over the world are being challenged and changed. Is it the harmonic convergence or are Baby Boomers worldwide undergoing a cosmic mid-life crisis all at once? Whichever it is, we can look for further changes in political structures, economic arrangements, and even (it is hoped by many of us) religious institutions and beliefs.

In order to survive—and even thrive—in this quickening pace of change and transformation, we will need to be willing to abandon the old where it no longer fits, embrace the new where it is appropriate, and integrate the best of what we know with the risk of attempting what is unknown.

Unlike the Laredo City Council, we will not find certainty in rigid adherence to legislated opinion. Progress, growth, and spiritual fulfillment only occur where there is compassion, commitment, and an openness to the moving of the spirit of God—wherever that movement may lead.

MICHAL AND CORITA

In 1969 (nearly a hundred years ago) I was having a prolonged philosophical interaction with my draft board over the unfairness (my word) of granting exemptions to seminary students while drafting the daylights out of law, business, social work, and other professional schools. (The II-S deferment ended with college graduation.) Our meeting generated more heat than light when I refused the exemption and I was contemplating my next move when I received a small tubular package in the mail.

You may remember (if you are over a certain age) that, in the '60's, posters and wall hangings of all sizes were in. Snappy one liners by McCluhan, King, Kennedy, Malcolm, Che, Ram Dass and others were colorfully emblazoned on sheets of paper with metal strips on top and bottom, suitable for hanging in hallways, dorm rooms, and on socially aware office walls. I opened the tube to fine a small but colorful 3x6 inch poster stating that "To be a Christian is to know that *all* the rules will be fair and that there will be *wonderful* surprises." Of course it was by Sister Corita, the colorful, singing, California nun (who twenty years later would be replaced by a raisin.)

The friend who sent it meant well, just as friends of dying patients mean well when they say not to worry and that everything will be fine. But even then, as much as I wanted to believe it, I sensed it was not true. The rules were not fair, or if they were, then somebody had forgoten to enforce them. My friend was wrong, as was Corita, and it did no good to sit around wishing things were different.

Later, in the penitentiary where I worked, I heard inmates constantly complain that the rules were not fair while at the same time not making the same requirement for *their* behavior. My response to them was that, though life was not fair, it was not okay for us to be unfair in return. You can imagine the popularity of such a position, and the alacrity with which it was believed and followed.

Now, twenty years later, my nine year old daughter, Michal, responds to my loud lament about some public political or financial inequity with "Life isn't fair, Dad." Does she know this because it is emblazoned on the invisible psychological posters viewed in our conversations at the dinner table and bedtime? Or does she intuit this from her own interactions with newspapers, classmates, and Calvin and Hobbes? In either case, she is right. I only hope that she gets the rest of the statement right as well, that it is important to be fair, act fairly, create fairness—*especially* in an unfair world.

The truth is that "To be a Christian is to know that the rules are *unfair*, that there will be wonderful surprises *and* devastating disappointments." It is to trust that God is with us in both, audaciously encouraging us to be fair in the very face of unfairness, weeping with us in our mourning, laughing with us in our joy.

Michal and Sr. Corita. Opposite ends of the spectrum. I do not know where Corita is now, but I wonder if she has discovered the wisdom of being 9 years old in America today.

"WHY DID GOD DO IT?"

Michal's bathroom is right next to my office at home, with a door connecting. Often when I am typing or working at my desk, she will take a moment from reading Calvin and Hobbes in the bath to let the question that just passed through her nine year old brain escape into the atmosphere, usually with the expectation that Dad will make a wise and reasoned reply, which of course is always forthcoming.

Why did God do it?" came the echoing voice from beyond the shower door, a pink and brown-rippled outline of one arm against the glass.

Since I have become an expert on children in the last two years, I know that one must tread lightly with such a query, as it may be related to anything from hurricanes to babies.

"I don't know, sweetie. Why *did* God do it?"

"No, Daddy." (A disgusted rebuff. I am not playing my part right.) "You're supposed to say `Why did God do *what?*"

"Okay." (Always the compliant father.) "Why did God do what?"

"Well, why did God go to all the trouble to *make* us if we just *die* at the end? I mean, what's the *purpose*, anyway?"

"That's a *good* question, sweetie." (I vow to read Calvin and Hobbes to check where this is coming from, then decide she has visited the hospital once too often.) "We'll talk about it after your bath, okay?"

"Okay, Dad." (Back to the comics and she'll forget she asked in twenty-five seconds or less.) "And Dad?"

"Uh-huh." (Already I have discarded the need for a reply.)

"I won't forget this one."

But she did. And I was temporarily off the theological hook as her mind raced on to the more mundane problems of getting the tangles out, brushing teeth and saying prayers.

I had been granted some time to carefully prepare a sage answer for the next time it comes up. And it will. It will come up for the rest of her life, whenever she doesn't get something, or doesn't perform well, or experiences loss, or celebrates a significant birthday, like ten, or thirty, or forty, or, like the man I talked with today, ninety.

The usual pat answers are found in the Old Testament in Micah: it is to "Do justice, love mercy and walk humbly with God." In the N.T. and most other religious books the answer is: "Love one another." Good standard texts, both. But why, then, do we think (whether at 9 or 90) that death somehow discounts that love and makes it worthless, purposeless, meaningless? Why, indeed, did God make us if we die at the end?

There are other answers: 1. It seemed like a good idea at the time. 2. God doesn't think death is a biggie. 3. It doesn't work that way. 4. God goofed.

I vote for 2. The question "Why did God do it?" is a nonsequitur. It doesn't follow. It assumes that one negates the other. Death negates life. Life negates death. When in fact neither negates the other. They cannot, because they are both of the same piece. They are not opposite ends on the continuum, but merely markers that flag two events on a long continuum that precedes the former and proceeds after the latter. And to God the continuum is eternally now.

So the answer to Michal's question is that God made us and we live and die. The purpose in between is to be, to be with one another, to be with God, to be here now, and to be in the eternal now, which is neither hastened by life, nor negated by death.

That's what I told her when the voice in the tub brought it up again the next night. And I will tell it to her time and time again throughout her life. I just hope her response is always the same. She smooched me a kiss through the glass, said, "Thanks, Dad", and then went back to her important bathtime reading.

THE FOURTH WISE MAN

(Nathan Brown Joslin is a five-year-old friend of mine.)

Dear Nathan:

Where did the year disappear to? Only twelve months ago you were just getting used to your baby sister and now, at age five, you are hiding in the closet (very well and very quietly, I might add) from my new little girl, Michal. Someday I will painfully remind you that you didn't like being kissed by girls—or at least pretended you didn't.

Perhaps it is true that the older I get the faster time flies. Anyway, as the Family Theologian, it is time for me to explain the meaning of Christmas to you once again. So this year I will tell you the story of *The Fourth Wise Man*.

You didn't know there were four? Sure there were. Although most people think there were only three and their names were Gaspar, Balthazar, and Melchior. But the Bible doesn't actually tell us their names or even how many there were, so there can be four if we want. And we do.

I don't know what the other three were named, but the fourth was named Mark, and he didn't start out being a wise man. In fact, at the time of this story, he was only 8 years old, and he was in charge of the camels on which the Wise Men rode. (He had a little camel of his own that wasn't old enough to have grown a hump yet. The little camel's name was Humphrey.)

Mark had a pretty good life for those days. The Wise Men had found him as a baby, abandoned and left by the road to die because he was *mute*. (That means that he could not talk, though he could hear.) They took the orphan boy, named him Mark, and raised him as their own. They fed and clothed him and taught him all their knowledge as they traveled around the desert from town to dusty town. In return, Mark cared for their camels, helped set up their tents, cooked their meals, and looked after their possessions.

One night, on a hill outside the holy city Jerusalem, the four of them sat around the crackling campfire drinking hot chocolate (with marshmallows in it) and looking up at the stars twinkling in the sky. Mark felt safe and secure huddled up in his thick wool blanket, listening to the three Wise Men talk about their current journey. They looked very intensely at each other as they planned how they would carry it out. From what he could understand, they had learned about a newborn king whom they very much wanted to see. Mark looked up in the sky at the huge star which they had been following for days and days. They explained that the star would lead them to the baby's birthplace, and that they were taking him some very precious birthday presents. The presents were *gold, frankincense,* and *myrrh.*

Mark shrugged his shoulders and the Wise Men knew he didn't understand. (One of them even said, "Do you have a question, Mark?") They told him that the gold was to represent the baby's kingship over the whole earth, (because every earthly king has objects made of gold). Frankincense (which is not the name of a monster, Nate, but is a sweet-smelling spice, like the cologne your Poppa wears sometimes) was to represent the fact that, when he grew up, he would die and be anointed with sweet spices. And myrrh was an ointment like that salve your Momma puts on you when you skin your knee. It was to represent that the baby would be a healing person in people's lives.

That last thing got Mark's attention. He pointed to his throat and shook his head. He had seen many healers on their journeys and none had ever been able to help him, though they had all tried one strange thing or another. The Wise Men smiled and told him that the baby could not heal his throat and give him a voice, and Mark looked very sad and disappointed. He liked listening to the deep voices of the Wise Men and wished some day to be able to share all the knowledge they had given him by teaching and talking to others.

The Wise Men filled his cup with fresh hot chocolate from the campfire (and another marshmallow) and told him that his job would be to take care of the gold, frankincense and myrrh for the rest of the journey.

Mark smiled and knew that he had been given a task of great trust and value. He vowed to watch the gifts very, very carefully.

The Wise Men travelled all night (with Mark and the gifts waddling along atop Humphrey) following the star toward the little town of Bethlehem. When day came they made camp and prepared to sleep so they would be ready to follow the star again the next night. A very tired Mark was the first to go to sleep.

He was also the first to wake up when night fell. And what he saw before his eyes made his heart beat wildly with fright! There, standing in front of him, were two huge men. One had a large sword in his hand and pointed it right at Mark's throat. The other was rummaging silently through Mark's backpack—where he *pulled out the packets of gold, frankincense and myrrh!* Try as he might, Mark's throat would just not produce a sound to warn the Wise Men. Seeing that he was mute, the two men grinned their evil grins as they tied Mark's hands and feet together and quickly departed from the camp, before the Wise Men would wake up.

Mark's eyes filled with tears and his head filled with anger about not being able to shout to wake the Wise Men. He felt terrible and knew that they would be horribly disappointed with him. Worst of all, they would not be able to take their presents to this baby king and might even blame Mark for losing their valuable gifts. And, without a voice, he could not defend himself or explain what happened.

In an instant, he knew what he must do. He grabbed the backpack with his teeth and dumped out its contents. Then he managed to get his knife in his mouth and saw through the rope tying his hands and feet. Next, he saddled up Humphrey and rode into the night. He knew that the Wise Men would have to go on without him, but he hoped they would not think he had stolen their precious gifts. In any case, he would explain later. Right now, he had to get those gifts back.

He knew the two men could not have gotten very far on foot. But then he saw other camel tracks in the sand. Obviously they had sped out of sight and over the dunes to get away with their stolen treasure. Mark knew that he would have to use all of the skills the Wise Men had taught him to retrieve the gold, frankincense, and myrrh to give to the baby king and to restore himself in the eyes of the Wise Men. He got down under Humphrey and looked at the other camel tracks. The depth and closeness told him not only their direction but also their speed. He remembered the Wise Men teaching him about the placement of the stars and realized these evil men were heading in exactly the opposite direction from him. He knew that he and Humphrey would have to hoof it to catch them and get back to Bethlehem in time!

And hoof it they did. They also stayed downwind (another trick from the Wise Men) so that no sounds or smells (remember, Humphrey *was* a camel) would reach the evil men and tip them off that Mark was close on their heels. Finally, after what seemed like hours, they spotted the men around a campfire in a distant clearing. But how would he find out where the gifts were kept? And how would he ever be able to retrieve them? What would the Wise Men tell him to do, he wondered? And then he knew that they would tell him to do exactly what seemed best in his own mind, which is exactly what made them so wise.

First, he and Humphrey crept as close as they dared to the men. Then, using the arithmetic the Wise Men had taught him, he calculated the distance to the campfire and figured out how hard he would have to throw a rock to land in the middle of it. He motioned for Humphrey to lie down at his feet (which is where we get the expression "toe the Mark,") so he could not be seen or smelled by the other camels. Then Mark picked up a large stone, aimed carefully, and hurled it in a perfect arc—straight into the middle of the campfire, where it knocked a burning stick of firewood out near the backpacks and bags of the men.

Mark watched as the two men scrambled to get one particular pack out of danger. (They thought the fire had just popped the log out.) "Good," he thought. "They have just told me where the gifts are hidden. All I have to do now is get them back!"

Humphrey looked at him as if to say "Impossible!" but Mark already had a plan. Just like Nathan, he had learned to hide very, very quietly so that, even if someone were just a few feet away (like you in that closet) they would never hear him or find him. So he tied

Humphrey's rein to a tree and slowly, quietly, one step at a time crept closer and closer to their campfire. The bushes shaded him for a while, but then he had to crouch down very small and crawl behind some rocks. There he waited and waited—without making a single sound.

As they began to fix their dinner over the campfire, Mark heard the men talking about where to sell the gifts to get money for them. He peeked around the large boulder and saw them putting a pot of soup over the fire to cook. Then he reached into his pocket and pulled out two objects—a large stone and a sleeping pellet from a kit the Wise Men had given him long ago. He waited until they had their faces away from him and then hurled the rock as hard as he could into the other side of the clearing.

Of course the two men jumped to their feet. They picked up their swords and charged into the dark bushes. As they did, Mark ran out to their campfire and dropped the pellet into the pot of soup! Then he raced back behind the rock, and sat, very, very still, just like a piece of stone, or Nathan in a closet.

The evil men returned to the clearing, threw down their swords in disgust and anger at not finding the source of the noise, and began to eat their dinner. They ate the whole pot of soup, and all this while— which seemed like hours and hours—Mark sat silently behind the rock, just a few feet away (which is where we get the expression "Marking time.")

Finally, he heard a "thud" and peeked around the

rock to find the two men lying flat out on the ground! Slowly, cautiously he moved from his hiding place into the open. He even poked one of the men to see if he was really asleep. Sure enough, the pellet had done its work. The men were fast asleep and would not wake up for two days.

Quickly Mark ran to the bulging pack and looked inside to find the gold, frankincense and myrrh. Just to be certain, he tied the men's hands and feet with strong rope, scattered the fire to make sure it was out and ran from the campsite back to the waiting Humphrey.

"Hurry, Humphrey!" he shouted in his head, and gestured with his arms, though no words would come from his silent throat.

Humphrey looked at him curiously and immediately seemed to understand, so he started off at a gallop through the bush and back into the desert toward Bethlehem. It was easy to know the direction, because of the huge star in the heavens above them.

After riding the entire night, Mark and Humphrey finally saw the outline of Bethlehem on the horizon. Morning was breaking and the star was fading, so, even though they were nearly exhausted, they had to hurry to find the place where the baby king had been born.

At first Mark couldn't believe it. It was a *stable* behind an inn. He looked around and around for a palace, for the Wise Men had said it was a baby *king*, and kings surely lived in palaces. But when they turned a corner and found the other camels belonging to the Wise Men, Mark was certain this was the place.

Mark took the pack with the gifts and knocked on the stable door. It was a weak little knock because he was so tired. When one of the Wise Men came to the door, he did not speak to Mark but grabbed the sack and closed the door in his face. Mark knew that they thought *he* had stolen the gold, frankincense and myrrh; he walked dejectedly back to Humphrey, who was lying on the ground with his hooves over his eyes.

Mark sat down, leaned against Humphrey, and wondered how he could tell them what had happened. Suddenly, he looked up and saw a *huge* angel. (Yes, Nate, the angel had a beard, cowboy hat and boots. It was Bubba! Remember him from last year?)

"Don't you worry none, little fella," Bubba said. "I saw it all. You and that baby in there have a lot in common, ya know. He's gonna be misunderstood all his life—and afterwards too. But you have done a brave job and kept the trust they put in you. And if they were *really wise* men, they would know that. So let me go have a little chat with 'em. I'll wise 'em up some." He rose in the air as Humphrey peeked out from under one hoof. "You and the critter wait right here."

Mark was so stunned he could not move. Humphrey was shaking enough for both of them. In a little while the barn door opened and a tall man came toward them. His name was Joseph. He took Mark by the hand and, grabbing Humphrey's rein, led them both into the stable.

Mark was amazed to see the three Wise Men kneeling down in front of a woman holding a tiny baby. On the ground in the hay before them were the gold, frankincense and myrrh. Mark stopped cold, pulling back from Joseph, and Joseph immediately understood.

"No, Mark," Joseph said. "We want you to come see the baby. His name is Jesus and you have already given him the greatest gift of all."

Mark looked up at him, curiously.

"Yes, it's true. The angel told us that you have given him the gift of your *courage.* If only others will do the same for him, the world really will be made better by his birth."

Humphrey nudged Mark and together they went to the baby. The woman (whose name was Mary) smiled at the boy and the camel. As the Wise Men looked on, Mark sat down beside her and she carefully handed the infant to him.

Looking into the baby's sparkling eyes, Mark thought of a hundred, no, a thousand things he wanted to say. And the baby looked back at him, blinking and wiggling his little arms in the swaddling cloths. Then the baby smiled (or maybe twitched) and Mark looked up at Mary. Without even thinking Mark *spoke*, in a soft, whisper thin voice that was barely heard: "He's...so...beautiful."

"Yes, he is, isn't he?" Mary replied.

It was then that he knew Mary had *heard* him speak—and that *he* had heard *himself!* He looked at the Wise Men, who were so astonished and happy that they were weeping and laughing all at once. (One of them even said "Mark! My word!" and that phrase is still being used today in situations of great surprise.) Humphrey bent down and licked Mark and the baby, as Mary patted the camel on the nose.

"I...I would like...to give him something...else," Mark said, plunging his hand deep into his pants pocket. He placed a small, wadded up pink object next to the three gifts left by the Wise Men. Joseph smiled and said, "When he is old enough, we'll give it to him, and tell him who it is from."

"Thank you," Mark said, as the Wise Men stood to leave. "But tell him not to use it all at once. It will last longer if he only uses a little at a time."

"We will tell him. And we will tell him about the courage of the boy who gave it to him."

One of the Wise Men added, "And tell him of the love that risks and heals and empowers—as it did this boy."

"He will tell the world of that himself," Mary said, waving as she watched them walk out the stable door, leading the camel.

Once outside, the three older men stopped Mark and, bending down, put a small, jeweled ring on his finger, for now there were *four* Wise Men. Just then, Humphrey snorted at them and turned his head to his back—where there was the beginning of a grown up camel hump! A huge, toothy smile beamed from his camel lips as the other three Wise Men helped Mark— *The Fourth Wise Man*—up on Humphrey's now lumpy back.

As they rode away in the cool morning of that First Christmas Day, Mark knew he would always remember the baby Jesus and those first words to shatter the dark silence. And, though Mark would never know it, Jesus would remember the four gifts given by the four Wise Men—gold for power, frankincense for anointing, myrrh for healing, and *bubble gum to remind him to play*.

Love,

Uncle Chuck

LITTLE THINGS DONE WELL

Debi *had* to go into a plain old French department store in the little town of Alencon. Europeans have the sensible habit of closing everything down from noon-2pm and we had just finished our hot chocolate at the patisserie when the cathedral bell announced the re-opening of the stores. After much maneuvering in the tiny streets, I actually found a spot in front of the store. I walked through it once with Debi and (having seen all one needed to see, of course) went outside to check out the area. When Debi came out with her treasures (three washcloths and a towel,) I announced the finding of St. Theresa's house, two doors up on this non-descript street. It turned out to be the real treasure.

An English-speaking nun toured us through and told us the story of this modern day saint who entered the convent at age 14 and died there at age 24. What was it she did to be canonized? Did she heal the sick, perform miracles, show great piety, or write deep religious tomes? None of the above. She did little things well. That's all. "Little things well." Ordinary tasks like washing and ironing and singing and praying and gracefully serving others and cheering people up.

In the house there are pictures of her at these tasks, with the explanation that that is what her peers remembered best about her, and their reason for requesting her canonization. It was really quite impressive. This St. Theresa of the Infant Jesus is renowned around the world now, missionary orders spawned from her name, intercessions aimed at her, petitions in her name—and all because of her love of service—simple things, little things done well.

The overwhelming feeling in that house is one of peace and respect. A little chapel has been built in the upper level for people to stop in and pray. It is simple, like Theresa Martin's works, and like the works of ordinary people all over the world—even those seemingly insignificant, little things done well where you are right now.

It is not in the magnificent, front-page accomplishments of the very few that the world is changed. It is in the unheard of, daily tasks of grace and unselfish service that suffering is relieved, that the lonely are cheered, that the sick are comforted. And it is not only in those ensconced in religious habits that do these deeds. You and I are responsible for doing them every day. It is your smile, your touch, your calm voice, your concerned question, your gentle direction, that makes a difference.

We may not be canonized for it, but it is perhaps enough to know that we have left this day better off than when we found it, and the people with whom we have interacted have been touched or welcomed or empowered or simply acknowledged by "little things done well."

"GOOD DEATH"

When is it okay to kill yourself? By the time you read this the topic will have been discussed by Donahue, Sally, Oprah, and Geraldo, (all of them relating the problem to sexual practices in the U.S. today).

The issue was raised dramatically when a 54 year old woman, diagnosed with early Alzheimer's, arranged to have herself hooked up to a "suicide machine" by a pathologist and pushed the buttons for a drug to kill her. In the next few days a New Mexico judge ruled that an alert and interacting quadriplegic could remove his respirator (with assistance) and die.

The word for this is euthanasia—literally meaning "good death." This way of dying is perceived by many people to be characterized by control (as opposed to helplessness), dignity (as opposed to the indignity of high tech death), timeliness (as opposed to both "natural" and mechanically assisted dying that seems interminable), and quality (as opposed to mere quantity of days). But others think it is hopeless (giving up any hope of miraculous recovery), selfish (demanding death on one's own terms), sacrilegious (God should choose when one dies), and wasteful (one should live out whatever days are left).

The healthcare establishment already practices what a friend of mine calls "tangential euthanasia." We knowingly and ethically give pain relievers which will reduce respirations and hasten death. We remove artificial interventions such as respirators, hydration, nutrition, antibiotics, dialysis and medicines, or continue other comfort measures that we know will allow death to occur. But, at least in our society, the question remains as to whether, and under what circumstances, one has the option of suicide when faced with death or disability. And the definition of suicide is changing. Is it suicidal, for instance, when diagnosed with a fatal illness (or incurable condition) to choose only comfort measures from the beginning, foregoing chemotherapy, radiation, medicines, surgery, or experimental procedures?

In the coming decade, we will have to debate these issues and come to consensus about them. Ought we to allow euthanasia at all? Under what circumstances? What qualifies as a futile condition? Need one be terminal, or incurable, or hopelessly disabled, or beyond a certain age? How might it be done? Should physicians administer the drug or oversee its use? What part will the legal and legislative systems play? What about the church?

Regarding this last question, it is interesting to me that polls indicate the more "religious" the person, the more opposed they are to euthanasia; because my own sense is that euthanasia does not usurp what some believe is God's prerogative. Instead that alleged prerogative is usurped by artificial interventions which prolong the dying process. If we are created to be free, then we are to use our God-given intellectual and emotional judgement to decide when our quality of life is no longer consistent with who we were and are. That same judgement may lead us to spare ourselves the indignities of a "natural death" and instead choose the "good" one.

SUGAR II —
THE GRIM GARAGE DOOR

How to put this delicately, that is the problem. Expired? Too imprecise; parking meters and library cards expire. Croaked? Inaccurate description and meant for another species; frogs croak. Died? Usually my favorite word due to its honesty, but not quite graphic enough here. Spent his tenth life? Closer, but not yet it. Met his end when face to face with The Grim Garage Door? That's it. That's what happened to Sugar the Cat.

Earlier in this volume you read the story of Sugar the Cat, the bane of my existence, getting himself locked in the garage of the vacant house next door for four days in the heat of summer. (My rescuing him from that proved only to be a stay of execution.) Since then he had become enamored of walking precariously on the roof—and jumping down to the top of the metal shed at 2 a.m. for the sole purpose of jolting my systole from Sleep mode to Rambo. He would also lounge on his furry grey back with one white paw dubiously dangling off the edge of the diving board just to raise my hopes that he would roll over in his dreamy kitty sleep and have to endure the indignity of yet another Chuck-rescue. He used up several more of his lives by stolidly ignoring the strafing of a local bluejay, picking on the senile drooly cat (whom I like) at 4 a.m., and regularly defacing my clean windshield with dusty paw prints.

But it was the garage that fascinated Sugar the most. Like a moth to a flame, he seemed drawn to its danger, challenged by its risks, destined to meet his demise there. He would sneak up the wooden folding stairs behind me and hide in the dusty recesses of its attic, crunching through the old fiberglass batting as if in deep crusty snow, refusing all entreaties to stop and needing to be rescued from his dangerous curiosity. Once, Debi and Michal heard meowing from the garage. Sugar was trapped in the attic, and when Debi pulled down the stairs (on which he stupidly stood) he unexpectedly shot down to the cement floor. Catapulted, as it were. Kamikaze kitty.

Sugar's affinity for the garage was matched only by my determination to keep him out of it. I daily chased, pulled, broomed and carried him from its hazardous hollows, including his recently acquired resting place atop the raised garage door.

The first time I saw him there (last winter) I thought he was funny. The second time, when I hit the button to close the door and saw him nonchalantly riding it backwards because he was too dumb to jump off, I speculated loudly and in the presence of witnesses that the fuzzy mental giant would probably meet his end in this fashion, since no one could tell when he was there. Eight months later he did, inadvertently startled from sleep by a descending door which he rode into kitty heaven. And just when we were beginning to get along. Really.

It was my job as The Dad and Professional Expert In These Matters to, uh, "retrieve" the cat, "take care of" the body, and "break the news" to our nine year old daughter Michal, who, knowing well my anti-feline affinities, looked at me intently for any sign of a smirk. There was none, and Sugar's silly, pesty, and dangerous deeds grew immeasurably in the retelling of them together, as is the case with nearly everyone.

Sugar lived his short, furry life on the edge (of the roof, pool and garage door.) He pushed the limits, was careless and risky, in need of affection and solitude, maddening and funny, and ultimately in the wrong place at the wrong time. In these ways he was sort of an Everycat, reinforcing to us the message that behavior has consequences, that life is too short (even with nine of them), that it is important to finish up unfinished business with loved ones daily and to live as best you can one pussycat day at a time. For you never know the day or the hour when the Grim Garage Door will move under you.

P.S. For the record, I will miss the little critter (sort of.) Also for the record, I really did *not* know that he was up there when I absently punched the button and drove down the street to work that morning. And I think it was his final ploy to arrange his demise so as to cast the shadow of blame in my direction.

AFTERLIFE

I suppose it started with the last of the Star Wars trilogy where, at the end of the movie, you see all the principal characters (including the "dead" ones) smiling and waving at Luke Skywalker. But now it has gathered steam and we are being deluged with the fact that BABY BOOMERS HAVE DISCOVERED THE AFTERLIFE. As they all (or is it *we* all?) plunge over the mid-life waterfall and see that we are aiming headlong toward The Inevitable, there is a desperate attempt (like swimming back up) to explain, foretell, or deny where we're heading. Thus we find appearing such movies as *FIELD OF DREAMS, ALWAYS, DEFENDING YOUR LIFE, GHOST, FLATLINERS, DEAD AGAIN* and other visual forays into the final future. Even the novelist John Irving, whom I usually admire for his wit and style, has written a description of his view down the falls in *A Prayer For Owen Meany*. Unfortunately, I think he got bonked by a rock on his way over.

Through the years I have been asked questions about the afterlife ranging from: "Do babies grow up there?" to "Does he or she know what I'm doing/thinking now and can they intercede or protect us?" to "What is resurrection?" And those questions, along with my own plunge over the Niagara of Life have led to the following thoughts:

1. We choose to spend eternity (from Now till Whenever) either in God's presence or out of God's presence; in eternal light or eternal darkness. We make that choice with every thought we have and every action we do. The choice is always open to us: now, when we die, and after death. The choice cannot be earned; eternity in light is a gift. Like a gift it must be accepted and wanted, or rejected and ignored.

2. Bodies grow and age. Spirit/matter/essence is eternal and ageless, so that when they meet they are always the same. Spirits continue to "grow" in their knowledge of God, a task which by definition takes eternity. Spirit is not superior to body (nor vice versa). Perhaps the body is of equal necessity in the body/soul journey, experiencing and learning things about God that cannot be learned in any other way (no matter how long that journey lasts).

3. Although the sentimental movies would have it otherwise, and some people report events to the contrary, I believe that there can be no physical interaction between spirit and life here, though interaction in terms of prayers, thoughts, and loving intentions certainly continue. Love is always stronger than death. But that plane of existence is so much broader, more inclusive and of such a different perspective as to make contact or intervention futile and pointless.

As we Baby Boomers (and others) plunge our way toward Golden Pond there will be further descriptions of what is waiting beyond it. Some guidelines are in order: 1. Beware of anyone claiming to have the absolute truth about any of this. There are no "right" answers, only reasoned speculation. 2. Take nothing literally; the important thing is how the metaphors (images) affect and direct our lives now. 3. Remember that, whatever we imagine the afterlife to be, it will probably be different, so it is important to have a good sense of humour about it. Given the rigid, judgmental, exclusive, wishful, and sentimental descriptions we have devised, I am certain that God does.

MICHAL'S WEDDING

Michal got married last week. She and I were driving over to a friend's house when, in the midst of playing with her bride doll, she said that when *she* got married it would be "to a nice, smart person you could trust who was sweet like Daddy" (of course.) And he would be, personality-wise, "in the middle between a guy with an earring and a nerd." (The obvious two ends of the desireable spectrum.) Nathan Joslin (two years her junior) would be best man because she liked and trusted him, her friend around the corner Jessica Sager was to be her maid of honor, her sisters in Indiana would all be in the wedding party and it would be at St. David's Church downtown because it was big enough. She had the cake catered, the groom could have a carrot cake if wanted, and the music ("a Mozart something") lined up and the guy's name was Timothy (safe because there are no such beings at school or church though there is a kid whose name begins with T of whom I am becoming suspicious.)

Marriage. Age 9. Aside from all the obvious developmental and imitative meanings (God help us when the hormones kick in,) I am struck again by the strong need in Michal and in all of us human beings to bond, to be a part of something, to belong, to securely trust someone else enough to allow them to know you at your best and worst and hope they still like you.

Marriage has been a traditional cultural symbol for that knowing and being known, and our relationship with God is often described in this metaphor. The Bible is replete with wedding stories—the parable of the marriage feast, the wedding at Cana—describing the interaction between us and God as one of celebration where the mundane (water) becomes precious (wine), where the bland becomes intoxicating. There is a sense of playfulness but also of commitment, of demand but also of forgiveness, of love that is romantic but also realistic, tough enough to endure the inevitable happenings that will excite, distract, and afflict us along the way of our journey together. But it is also true that new ways to interact are developing as we move into this decade of the 90's and beyond. Different kinds of relationships with varying degrees of bonding and commitment are emerging between long term friends, between people of the same or opposite sex and, as our population gets older, between persons of varying ages. When I commented recently to my 86 year old Dad that he and my Mom were outliving all their friends and therefore might want to consider moving to Austin to be near us, he got an ironic smile on his face and said, "Yes, but the problem is we're making new ones." On a larger scale, these new styles of relationships are developing between individuals and organizations, and even between nations.

I told Michal that I was certain she would make good choices in the persons she would go out with, be friends with, and eventually marry (or grok or plotz or whatever they're calling it in the next century.) That is of course a brilliant observation on my part, and it is a fervent prayer and admonition for her to do so. But I want her to know she is okay either single or married, that there are many kinds of bonds she will form throughout her life, and that the most important one will be the eternal one she develops with God as God is revealed to her, seeks her out, stands with her through all the passages—joys, sorrows, deaths, re-births—in her (hopefully) long life. It is, I believe, that relationship that will sustain all of her other ones.

Now all I have to do is keep my eye out for a guy named Timothy—who will probably be a nerd *with* an earring.

JOSEPH'S LINES

"Last year Joseph messed his lines up," Michal said over breakfast as I queried her about what she wanted to do in the Christmas Pageant. Two pancakes later I learned that she did not want to do *anything* in the play because it was boring and the angels only got two lines and you had to be in the fifth grade to be Mary and it was *not* fun. After much discussion with her Sunday School teacher, Michal decided to be the caretaker of the "animals"—little kids aged 3-5 who dress up like critters of all kinds. (Last year one was a tiger complete with whiskers, which prompted another kid in the audience to exclaim "MOM, WERE THERE *TIGERS* IN THE BARN?" just when one of the Wise Men was supposed to say something profound.)

Michal is just learning that people (of all ages, much to her surprise) make mistakes, that life is not always fun or fair, but that lots of negotiation can sometimes get your needs met, if you persist. (Like the 60's song "You can't always get what you want, but if you try, sometimes, you get what you need.") And the holidays are the perfect setting for that learning.

We realize at this time of year the unfairness of the world, the losses we have had and the losses we can expect, the effects of aging upon our physical abilities, the blows dealt to those we love. We are aware of our own mistakes with one another, and of the mistakes people have made toward us (in the old days that used to be called "sin"—very unfashionable now, though.) We are told daily about the things we should want that will, of course, make us smell better, look better, feel better, act better, be better all of which implies that there is something drastically wrong with us the way we are. And we are told that there should be quick solutions, usually by means of power of one person over another.

So into this world of mistakes, unfair and unfun circumstances, and personal deficiencies comes the Jesus child. He comes not to fix it, not to assure that there will be no mistakes, nor to make it fair or fun, but to BE with us in the midst of it, talking with us, listening to us, helping us to know and to receive what we NEED, encouraging us to risk all things to get what we need. For what we need is one another, and that requires accepting, forgiving, welcoming, renewing, changing, helping—all the things, you will note, that you can almost never do alone, without help, without seeing that Jesus child beside us doing them with us.

No wonder we greet him with cries of joy and welcome.

So I will watch the pageant this year, and in the midst of inappropriate baby animals (attended and corralled by Michal,) diseased-looking sheep, scruffy angels, raggedy wise men, a 5th grade Mary and a crowd of harried parents, I will be grateful that that baby is wailing again—and wait for Joseph to get his lines wrong.

THE INNKEEPER NAMED
HAROLD

(Nathan Brown Joslin is a First Grade friend of mine.)

Dear Nathan:

Before I begin this year's story, your Uncle Chuck (the Family Theologian) has a confession to make. I am certain your Momma and Poppa haven't told you before now but you are in first grade and old enough to hear it. Just like the Coyote and Road Runner, there is Uncle Chuck and Bubba. You may remember Bubba—the six foot, 280 pound Texas angel—from the stories of the last two years. But what you didn't know is that he is a personal friend of mine. My daughter Michal knows him, as he often gives her a sermon for me to deliver instead of the one I have written, and she stands up in church when I can't find mine and hands his to me to read. It is very embarrassing. And Bubba likes it.

So now you know. Uncle Chuck talks to an angel named Bubba. Actually, Uncle Chuck *listens* to Bubba, who shows up at the oddest times. Like when I started writing your letter.

There I was, sitting at the typewriter, wondering what to tell you about Christmas this year. I've told you about the Donkey Named Glory, the Star Named Tink, the Shepherds And Bubba, and The Fourth Wise Man. What was left to tell? As I sat, scratching my head and frowning, I suddenly heard a deep voice in the chair behind me.

"Tell him about the Innkeeper named Harold!"

I nearly fell off my seat as I whirled around to see that huge angel in my favorite leather reclining chair, with a Sprite in one hand and a bowl of popcorn in the other. His large wings were draped over the back of the chair.

"BUBBA!" I exclaimed. "What are *you* doing here?"

"A fine greetin' boy! A fine greetin'. Why, I even had to make my own popcorn and get my own drink. And me on a mission of mercy, too."

"Mission of mercy?"

"Yep. I was makin' my rounds and saw you down here fumblin' around, tryin' to spin a story for that young'un...so I knew I'd better drop in and tell you what really happened, so Nathan wouldn't be so confused."

I resisted the temptation to dump the bowl of popcorn on his head. The last time I did something like that he sat on me 'till he finished his story. Besides, I'd never heard this one before.

"And I suppose you know what really happened because you were there?"

"Does a dog have fleas, boy? Of *course* I was there!"

Bubba lowered his normally booming voice. "But I was in-cog-nito. I was dis-guised!"

I pointed to his large belly. "As what—an overfed water buffalo?"

"Very funny, boy. Very funny," he said, ignoring me to get on with his story. "I was disguised, for your information, as a weary traveler lookin' for a room. That's how I know about Harold the Innkeeper."

"You mean you got to that inn before Joseph and Mary?"

"That's right, boy. Old Harold refused me a room before he refused them one. That's how I know there was no room at the inn, and what Harold's problem was."

I propped my feet up and leaned back in my chair. "Okay," I said. "You've got my attention. Tell me the story."

"Thought you'd never ask, son," Bubba said, taking a drink and swallowing a handful of popcorn. "It was like this...Every now and then we angels dress up like you humans and check things out for the Boss, like how kind or helpful or generous you are."

"I guess I blew it on the popcorn, huh?"

"Don't worry. I'll give you another chance later." He munched down more of the fluffy stuff. "Anyway, I was checkin' out some of the people there in Bethlehem, when I wandered into the inn run by Harold."

"Last name?"

"Daye. And he named it after his wife whose name was, uh...Holly."

"The Holly Daye Inn?" I groaned.

"Catchy, huh? But try not to interrupt me, boy...Now, where was I?"

"You were checking in to the Holly Daye Inn."

"Yeah. And I went up to the counter and there was Harold the Innkeeper looking upset and dejected. It seems that one of his twin boys—John—had wandered off somewhere and hadn't been seen for days. Holly was very upset, and Harold was trying his best to keep the inn running at full tilt and look for the boy, too."

"But Harold was frazzled. Worn to the bone. Stressed to the max. Circuits fried. So he wasn't in too cordial a mood when I rang the bell on the desk. I noticed that a couple of mail slots behind the desk had keys in them and so I was surprised when he told me there were no rooms available. I guess he looked me over when I came in and decided that, since I wasn't wearing the best of clothes, he could get a higher price for those rooms from one of the many wealthy travelers passin' though Bethlehem that weekend. When he told me those rooms belonged to his family and he couldn't rent them, the little boy (about Nathan's age) standing behind him peeped his head out and tugged on his father's shirt. He had a mop of black hair that nearly covered his huge brown eyes."

"Daddy?"

"Don't bother me now, Amahl. I'm working."

"But Daddy...those rooms...?"

Harold the Innkeeper glared at his son. "They are full, Amahl. Now go help your mother in the kitchen, and keep an eye out for your brother."

"Amahl left and Harold apologized for the boy. He explained they had all been on edge since John disappeared two days before—especially since a Spanish circus had passed through town at the very same time. In fact, John had last been seen playing with one of the circus kids on the edge of town.

"Anyway, Harold said there was no room in the inn. Either he wasn't a very good liar, or he remembered that you should always treat strangers well because they might be angels in disguise, because he did soften a little and recommended a flophouse down in the other end of town."

"What happened then? Did Joseph and Mary show up?"

"Don't rush me, boy. I'm runnin' out of popcorn."

I quickly made another batch and returned with enough to last us both long into the night.

"Thanks, son. Now, as I was sayin'...uh...what was I sayin'?"

"You were leaving the Holly Daye Inn because there was supposedly no room, but you didn't tell me where you went."

"Oh, yeah, sure, I remember now...I was leavin' the inn. But you know, I got to worryin' about poor old Harold, tryin' to make ends meet and distracted about poor little John and all...and then there was that other cute little fella...."

"I thought you didn't like kids...?"

"I don't! Cain't stand the little curtain climbers! But this kid was tuggin' on his Daddy and lookin' so pitiful...Well, I didn't have much time to think about it as it turned out."

"John came back?"

"Will you *hush* and let me tell this? Stuff some of that popcorn in yore face or somethin'."

I sighed and leaned back in the chair.

"Now here's what happened. And lissen up good, 'cause you'll have to tell it to Nathan when I'm through."

I nodded.

"Just as I was leavin' the place I heard the 'clomp, clomp' of hooves on the cobblestone street leadin' up to the inn. I hung back in a doorway and watched a very tired Joseph leading the poor old donkey with an agonizing Mary on its back. They saw me standin' there and asked if I could help. I said (and I was later quoted in a famous movie): 'I don't know nothin' about birthin' babies.' But it turned out they just wanted directions to the nearest inn and I pointed them to Harold and Holly's place—knowing what would happen."

"Why did you do that? Why didn't you just send them someplace else?"

Bubba sat forward in the chair and looked at me, wide-eyed. "You don't mess with *symbols* boy!"

"Symbols? What's so symbolic about being refused at the Holly Daye Inn?"

"Boy, where *did* you go to seminary?" Bubba asked, wolfing down another handful of popcorn and washing it down with the rest of the Sprite. "The *symbolism* is that, for the rest of Jesus' life—beginning with his even trying to find a place to BE BORN—there would be 'no room in the inn' of people's lives for him. Either they're too busy, or too upset, or too tied down by obligations, or too scared, or too distracted by others, or too worried about takin' a chance and being associated with him (he's not always well-dressed, you know), or like Harold, hoping to fill their lives with something better than Jesus, or maybe even thinking Jesus wouldn't stay there with them if they DID invite him in. For whatever reason—from the very beginning until right up to now—there's been no room in the inn of people's lives for Jesus." Bubba looked satisfied with his explanation and leaned back in his chair. "...and *that's* the symbol, boy."

I looked skeptically at him. "And you expect Nathan to understand...?"

"He's a smart boy. You just tell him the world's been trying to keep Jesus out from the time Jesus was born. Nathan knows how it feels not to be wanted in a game or by friends. All kids do. Especially when you've got a baby sister." Bubba nodded his head. "Trust me. I know kids...."

(I decided I would have to discuss this at length with you, Nate, over a Shiner milkshake or two, and I let Bubba continue.)

"So you directed them to the inn?"

198

"Yes. And Harold the Innkeeper did it again. He told them there was no room. But—and I know this because I used my special angel-hearing to listen to their conversation—Amahl tugged on his Daddy's shirt again and pointed to the pregnant Mary with a look of sadness in his eyes.

"'Daddy', he said, '...How about the barn out back? I'll go clean out a spot for them.' So Harold took compassion on them and said they could stay in the barn, and Amahl went out and helped them get settled as best they could. He scattered the pigs and chickens and cows into other stalls and got the warmest one ready for the tired man and the slowly moving woman. He even put down some fresh straw for them to lie upon."

"I think I know the rest of the story, Bubba," I said confidently.

"No you don't."

"Yes I do."

"No you don't!"

"Yes I do!"

"Your problem, boy, is that you keep forgettin' who the angel is around here," Bubba said, staring at me. "And if you know the rest of the story—tell me how John got back?"

"John who?"

"How can you know the rest of the story if you cain't even keep the characters straight?" he glared at me. "John the twin brother!"

I thought a second, tapped my foot and raised my eyebrows. Then I said: "So continue."

"Thank you very much," Bubba said sarcastically. "Now, before I was thrown off track, I think that Joseph and Mary had just gotten into the barn."

I added, " And Amahl had cleaned a stall for them where a couple of cows had been lying so the straw was still nice and warm."

"How did you know that?" Bubba asked.

"Elementary, my dear Bubba," I grinned. "Amahl's a nice kid, just like Nathan. He'd do something like that."

"Well, it just so happens that he did," Bubba said reluctantly. "And that's when I knew it was time for me to go find his brother."

"Why?"

"Well, I figured that maybe, with a little help, that family could come around. And, after all, Harold the Innkeeper did let Mary and Joseph have a place to go to have the baby," Bubba smiled. "Matter of fact, no sooner did Mary lie down on the hay than that baby started to be born."

"How did you know where to look for John?"

"Simple, boy," Bubba grinned. "Harold said he was last seen with the circus kids. So I unfolded my wings from under the cape I wore and took off in the night sky to find their encampment. It was easy to see because there was such great starlight coming from one special star shining down over Bethlehem that night. I found the camp about 20 miles away and softly landed behind one of the circus tents. I went invisible and slowly walked through the camp, looking at the children. It wasn't until I came to the very last tent that I saw him. The other kids were calling him by the name they used in Spanish—'Juan' instead of 'John.'

"Since they were just going to sleep I waited a few minutes until all the lanterns were out and their breathing stilled. Then I scooped up Juan and took off into the sky once again. He woke up once but thought he was just dreaming and slumped back into the blanket in my arms.

"Just as I landed by the stable door, the cry of a little baby broke the silence and the darkness of the night. I don't know how to explain this to you, boy, except to say that it was like a light that came into the world all of a sudden-like, a light that made everything look different; sorta like Nathan hidin' under the covers of his bed and turnin' on a flashlight—except that this light was permanent, and no matter how dark it got, this light would always be there, not lettin' anybody ever again be in total darkness."

"And John woke up?"

"Yeah, he did. He woke up and went into the barn where his brother Amahl was sitting cross-legged watching the baby Jesus and Mary and Joseph all bundled up together. The two brothers hugged and looked at the baby and John told his brother how he had run away to join the circus, but it wasn't all it was cracked up to be and he was glad to be home—though he wasn't exactly sure how that had happened.

"Then they both went and woke their parents and pulled them, crying and laughing, back into the barn to see the newborn baby Jesus. Their parents fell to their knees and prayed a prayer of thanks for the safe return of the son. And, because I'm an angel, I knew that the Boss was glad that they had provided a safe place for His son to be born, too."

As Bubba sat back looking satisfied with himself, I quickly scribbled a few more notes on my pad so I could write this all down for you, Nathan. Then I looked up to ask Bubba another question that had occurred to me.

But he was gone, the popcorn bowl was empty and the Sprite bottle was lying on its side. Bubba had finished what he had come to do and was off to take care of his other chores. He did leave a note, though. It said, "Whatever you do, boy, don't call this story 'Christmas at the Holly Daye Inn.'" So I didn't. I called it "A Letter to Nathan" just like every other year. I hope you like it. And I hope you will remember to treat strangers as though they were angels in disguise—because Bubba may come to visit you personally some day to tell you more about the story of the baby Jesus and the first Christmas.

Love,
Uncle Chuck

P.S. Later that night I got to wondering how Bubba knew that the boy in the tent was really John with the light so dim and Bubba's eyes not being what they used to be a few hundred years ago. The next morning I found a note on my desk that read: "Simple, boy. When you've seen Juan—you've seen Amahl!"

WAR

I knew when I became Michal's Daddy that there would be some difficult times ahead for both of us. I knew, or I quickly found out, that I would have to work through with her the problems of bedtime and homework and chores and sleepovers and picking up her stuff and feeding the stupid cat, and eventually (God help us) adolescence and boys and dating.

In our relatively short time together we have covered a lot of territory, she and I, and we have forged from our laughing and yelling and crying together a relationship of trust, and open questioning and honesty and, I am embarrassed to admit, admiration. She expects me to be able to fix her bike, put her Barbie's leg back on, make her computer work, and walk her safely back to bed and tuck her in when she has a bad dream or the thunder gets too rumbly. Most of all she expects me to be able to answer any complex historical, psychological, or theological question clearly and in a few words of under three syllables. To all of these events, when we are finished, she smiles that Dad-tolerating grin of hers and pronounces: "That's what Dad's are for!" as she bounces off to the next adventure.

But last night, after her prayers that the people under the Congress Avenue Bridge would have a warm blanket and the children in Iraq would be safe, she asked me something I may not be able to answer with my usual flippant confidence. She was unusually quiet all night, especially after the announcement that The Wonder Years would be interrupted by Operation Desert Storm, so the thoughts must have been cooking for a few hours. Then, finally, in the hug following the prayer, when my face was next to hers, she asked me in her sleepy soft but utterly serious voice: "Daddy, why is there war?"

"That's a good question," I said—my usual response for buying some time. "I wish I knew the answer to that, Michal. My best guess is because there are differences between people about how to live, and because we as a world are still pretty stupid about how to solve our conflicts, and because we don't know much about peace, and because we like to consume and are largely unwilling to conserve, and because we don't yet see each other as brothers and sisters in one world."

Michal listened as intently as she could, given the subject and the hour. I could see she was still worried, so I hugged her again, smooched her forehead and patted her foot under the quilt as I left the room. "No matter what happens, Michal," I said, "I love you and I'm glad you're my daughter."

"I love you too, and I'm glad you're my Dad." Long pause. "And are you going to be right next door typing in your office on the computer?" she said, hopefully.

"I'll be right where you can hear me, Michal. Good night."

This is my third war. It is Michal's first and it has touched her deeply, indelibly. In the steady chipping away of innocence that we call growing up, this has been a painful chunk of loss. My guess is that that is true for all of us here. We had hoped, with the events of the last year, that perhaps we had outgrown war, decided to settle our differences with reasoned resolution, building new international cooperation and interdependence. But apparently that is not yet true for all of us in the world.

And so we come here today as we have done in other crises, wondering what to do, and what to think about this, filled with feelings of worry for those we love, some of us with concern for those we fight against, feelings of sadness and wonder how the need for war serves us still, feelings of support for the allied troops, and worry that self righteousness on both sides will spill over into future wars.

And, after we have prayed our prayers for peace, and for safety for our loved ones, and for the children in all the affected countries, and for the folks under the Congress Avenue Bridge, with weary voices just like Michal's we ask God: "Why is there war?"

"That's a good question," God responds, in God's usual way of stalling for time. "Because you do not see the world the way I do; because you do not see each other as I do; because you worship other gods than me and you expect me to fix your bikes and put the legs back on your Barbies and make your computers work—and all I can really do is to walk you back to your room and be with you until the nightmare is over. I can cry with you and worry with you and be with you in your fear and anger, and forgive and welcome and comfort the hurt."

And perhaps that is enough. Perhaps it is for us to work for peace in our own lives and our own work and our own families and our own schools and our own city—so that that may translate into peace in our own world.

It will undoubtedly be some time before the conflict in the Gulf is over. Each of us will have and fears and angers and hopes and feelings of loss and sadness before it is done. Through it all it is important to hear God saying to us: "Whatever happens, I love you very much and I'm glad you are my sons and daughters." And it is important to respond "I love you too and I'm glad you're my God."

Finally, it will be important to remember that God is nearby in God's office typing busily away as we move together through this long and painful night, saying "I'll be right where you can hear me."

RESURRECTION

Nobody knows what happened after Jesus was crucified. A lot of people have been making claims about it for 2000 years, claims which range from "absolutely nothing" to "total bodily restoration from death." As with most things, my guess is that the truth lies somewhere in between, though to say so is dangerous territory, territory over which wars have been fought, people murdered, beheaded, burned, publicly flayed and defrocked. But what the heck, it's Easter. Let's go for it.

We know with some certainty (documented by other historians of the time who were not Christians, like Josephus) that Jesus was crucified and died by suffocation. To suffer three hours on a cross meant dying one breath at a time, no matter how hard you pushed up on the small platform with your feet. The person who wanted to break Jesus' legs was being kind in attempting to hurry the process.

When he was taken from the cross Jesus was entombed above ground, the earth in that area being unable to sustain subterranean interments. After that the story is written by those wishing to record its significance before too much was forgotten; the earliest account (Mark) being 60-70 years after the fact.

What is interesting is that the Gospels audaciously record the first witnesses not believing a word of it. The women who found the tomb empty ran to tell the disciples and were met by blank stares from incredulous faces. None of them expected it, and none accepted it. Even later, on the road to Emmaus, two disciples reportedly walked with Jesus and told him the story of the crucifixion and didn't recognize him until "he broke bread" with them. Then there are the instances of Jesus' "appearance" to disciples, where he is greeted with a mixture of astonishment and disbelief.

So what happened? What happened to turn a group of unorganized, disbelieving, frightened people into a force that changed the course of the world and still affects every one of us socially, culturally, psychologically and spiritually?

Resurrection happened.

In some way, probably totally different from anything we could imagine, they had an encounter with Jesus, with Jesus' spirit, or with a personage that they took to be Jesus, and the very best word that their language had that could attempt to bear the description of that encounter was—"resurrection."

We see resurrection all the time. The ebb and flow of the seasons, the healing of patients, the births and deaths in our families, the changes in our relationships with each other, forgiveness, mercy, acceptance, growth, love, renewal all are our current words for it. That we believe it can happen undergirds our commitment to all kinds of societal programs from emergency rooms and substance rehabilitation, to probation and poverty programs.

The amazing thing is not that the disciples experienced encounters with Jesus as "resurrection" after death. The amazing thing is that we all experience "resurrection" continuously throughout our lives. The function of religion, liturgy and Easter celebration is to remind us that the important thing is not surviving death, but surviving life, sustaining its ebb and flow together again and again and again.

CHRIST JESUS CHRIST

I had not planned to go to church that morning. I thought maybe I could sneak one week off and just go to Sunday School (which I was teaching), or at least sleep in and go to the 9a.m. service. But no. Children (I have learned) are creatures of habit and they continue to expect we will be also. We normally go to the 7:30a.m. service because it "doesn't have all that annoying music and it's shorter." So at 6:30a.m. I was greeted by smiling braces and two bunnies announcing it was time to get moving and go to church as usual.

Michal always has to sit in the second to the front pew so she can see the show and occasionally wink at her friends doing the service—which means that everyone *else* is behind us and can see and hear her. Being nine, she quickly picks up on Things That Don't Seem Quite Correct and announces them at the very time they are happening to whomever happens to be around. Thus as the lay reader stood and read from Paul's letter to the Ephesians, Michal pointed to the words in my book and, forgetting her "church voice," said aloud, "They got his name wrong!"

"Huh?" I roused from early service somnolence.

"Here," she pointed. "They got Jesus' name wrong!"

"No, its..."

"It's *supposed* to be 'Jesus Christ' and they've got it backwards! How could they do that?"

At this point the entire congregation had completely ignored the lay reader and were checking *their* books to see if it was wrong there, too.

"No, Michal," I said in my best church voice and red face. (What's black and white and red all over?) "It's okay that way. In fact, that's the *right* way to say it."

"But, Daaaad..."

(The priest was now checking *his* book...)

"Sssshhhh....I'll explain it at breakfast."

"Great!" she said, referring, I am sure, to the breakfast and not the explanation. And with that word we were allowed to continue the service.

Over pancakes she learned that "Christ" is a title like "King" and not a last name, thus properly coming first, as in "Christ Jesus." Paul got it right and the rest of us get it wrong.

Now the problem here is familiarity, assuming we know more than we do. In social situations it is considered polite not to call people by their first names unless invited or until we "know them well enough." Yet we use Jesus' name with frequency and call God's name as if they both lived next door for twenty years. And while that is real folksy and homey of us, we need to at least ask if it is not a tad presumptuous.

We make the same assumptions in healthcare. Someone tosses out the word "cancer" and we presume to "know" what it means; or "heart attack," or "head injury," or "schizophrenic," or whatever our specialty may be. We have gone over the same territory so often that the story is familiar and therefore less attended to than if it were new.

For the Hebrews, the concept of naming was a powerful one. If you knew the name of someone, it was implied that you knew pretty much about him. If you could name the evil or the disease, it was assumed that you had power over it or could understand it. Thus, when coming across God's Hebrew name (Yahweh) in the Bible, Hebrew readers would not presume to say the name of the unknowable; instead they say or read "Adonai" which means "Lord." Some Jewish friends of ours do not presume to write or read that name in English either, and so write "G-d" to convey the sense of transcendence and reverence.

So this morning when Michal alerted the congregation that Jesus' name was a typo, it occurred to me that she was on to something about Easter. We zip through Lent, through Holy Week, through Good Friday and past the painful, writhing death on the cross to the joy and rebirth of Easter assuming we know the events, the characters, the ending, and the meaning of it all. Been there. Done that. Next item.

It is only a careful reading of the story (as if it were new and interesting) that conveys to us the fear, the disillusionment, the despair, the extensive disbelief of everyone from Jesus to the disciples and the (literally) "incredible" surprise and astonishment of what they called "resurrection" because they had no better word for what they experienced. Of course, to read it this way is to be vulnerable to learning things we might not wish to learn, which would upset our stereotypes like the tables in the temple, demand from us different behaviors, bring us to give up preciously held secure religious and secular beliefs about who we are and who God is.

Thanks to Michal's astonished outburst, I will check my book more closely this Holy Week and be open to a different reading than my stereotypes had permitted before. Ironically, she was right. We get Jesus' name wrong all the time. Maybe this Easter I'll let him tell me what it really is.

EARS

I sat in church thinking about ears. That is an improvement over what I often think about in church, which is breakfast, because my wiggling, smiling, watch-checking daughter is giving me that "Where are we going to eat?" look. I got onto ears by glancing at the stained glass window and thinking that saint whoever-it-was had enormous ones. Unfortunately, I then compared those in the window to the lady sitting in front of me.

No contest.

When I was a kid going to the early early service just like Michal goes with me, my Dad used to swear he could get the lady sitting in front of him to scratch her ear just by staring at it. We would have contests to see who could do it first. He always won. We were very devout Episcopalians, you can tell.

But the ear I was really thinking about was my own. On a recent routine doctor's visit a nurse stuck something in it and took my temperature. That is correct—took my *temperature*. I was stunned by this action. I was totally unprepared for it. I expected the routine method of disposable tips connected by a spiral wire to a digital-read out that took all of about thirty seconds. What I got was a one second probe that gave an accurate reading instantly.

It put my mind into warp speed. In that one second, I felt the Berlin wall fall, the Soviet Union dissolve, apartheid die out in South Africa, and all remaining hostages be released. The world was becoming a different place all around me, and this quantum leap in technology that had caught me entirely off guard was symbolic of it. If this kind of technological change was possible, what was possible in the rest of healthcare?

Could we imagine a system of care giving where the patient merely showed a card and never saw a bill? Where immunization, prenatal care, well baby care, and nursing home care were provided as part of the system? Where invasive surgery was virtually unknown and unnecessary? Where prevention received as much funding as acute care? At the rate of speed at which things are changing, all of these things seem possible in our lifetimes.

And then, as I glanced back at the stained glass window, I wondered what the equivalent change would be for the Church? The four things determining what the Church does are: Scripture, Tradition, Reason, and Experience. Our experiences of the world today have changed and are continuing to change. Our reason tells us new things about the universe. Political, economic, and military industrial traditions are tumbling to make way for new ways of cooperating never thought possible. And Scripture is being interpreted in the new light from these changes.

What if the Church is the next bastion of culture to make a quantum leap into the present and future? What would happen? Will we develop a new understanding of who Jesus was? Of the sacraments? Of our theology of what the prophets and the patriarchs and the apostles and the entire history of the Church were and are about? Perhaps even of what *all* religions are about—together? What if the Church is the last Berlin Wall to fall? What will we find waiting to emerge from its rubble?

Michal nudged me and we went up to the altar rail to take Communion. The world she was growing into would be radically different than the one I knew. It was exciting—and scary. I was glad we held hands on the way back to the pew. I hoped we would still be holding hands when the Holy Spirit blew through the ancient corridors and created a new church, a new health care system, a new theology, a new world.

We passed the window with the saint I'd been watching, and I secretly whispered something to Michal before we sat back down.

In a minute the lady in front of us scratched her left ear.

THE LAST LETTER TO NATHAN

(Nathan Brown Joslin is a seven-year-old friend of mine.)

Dear Nathan:

It is *that* time of year again, and many things have changed. Family schedules have been rearranged around work and time off for your Mamma and Papa. The lovely little Lillian Ross is talking up a storm, much to your dismay, and has earned from you the hilarious nickname of "Ross the Boss." Buster is no longer a poopy puppy but is full grown and demanding your attention; and poor, ancient Rita finally made her terribly difficult journey into kitty heaven. You look like a big leaguer in your baseball outfit, complete with socks and cap; and you are hitting home runs and catching fly balls, running the Fun Run with your Papa and me without stopping, and sounding more grown up every time I see you.

So things are changing, endings have to happen before new beginnings can occur. This is the Last Letter to Nathan because it is time for an ending and a new beginning. I started writing these annual letters to you when you were seven months old, Nate, and now am writing this last one when you are seven *years* old. There's some symmetry in that, if not coincidence; that is to say, it fits. During this time I have endeavored, as The Family Theologian, to explain Christmas to you each year. In addition to the first two letters, I have told you the stories of The Donkey Named Glory, The Star Named Tink, The Angel Named Bubba, The Fourth Wise Man, and The Innkeeper Named Harold. And all of those stories led up to the most important one of all, the one I'm going to tell you this year, Nathan; the one that will (along with the others) carry you through the rest of your life, remind you of why we bother to celebrate this holiday at all, and provide comfort and meaning when you are feeling uncertain and alone in the midst of changes and endings in your life, which will happen all the time.

This year the story is about *The Baby Named Jesus.* It is a true story and all the events are accurate and factual, just like *all* of Uncle Chuck's stories, because he gets his information from Bubba the Texas Angel who was, in fact, actually there.

One day a long, long, time ago, God strolled across heaven, enjoying the bright sunshine and the fluffy clouds, and smiling and nodding politely at all the other spirits up there who just like to be around him and listen to him hum or whistle or sometimes even sing. God was in a particularly good mood that morning because he had gotten up early and jogged while the sun rose and then had a great breakfast and a shower and felt really pleased with the way things were going in the universe. He was whistling a tune he had heard in the Peruvian rainforest, and trying to match it with something from Mozart, and the result was really quite nice, when one of the angels who had been gone for a couple of days came flapping furiously up to God, sweating and smelling like Luling oilfields in August.

"You've got to *do* something, Boss!" the angel exclaimed.

God stopped in his tracks and looked at the angel like he was out of his eternal mind. "At the risk of stating the obvious," God said, "I already *have* done something." He pointed to the earth. "We are talking pigs, chickens, cows, birds, plants, and even people, here. Or isn't *that* enough?"

"But that's the problem..."

"The *problem?*" God said, his wide eyes looking puzzled. "There is a *problem?*" His huge voice rolled like thunder across the heavens.

The angel suddenly realized that maybe he had just stepped into something that was going to be hard to get off of his cowboy boots. (Yes, Nate, of course the angel was Bubba.) But he persisted anyway because it was very important. "Well," Bubba said, "..as a matter of fact, God...yes there *is* a problem."

"Great..." God continued, sitting down on a large grey cloud with his elbows on his knees and his head in his hands to think a minute. "What did I forget this time? Or are they still complaining about mosquitos and flies? So I messed up a little..."

"It's not the mosquitos or the flies...and I don't think it's something you forgot."

"Well, *that's* a relief. What *is* it then?"

Bubba cleared a hole in the clouds in front of God. "Actually, it's something *they* forgot." He pointed down to the earth. "Look..."

So God looked down and this is what he saw:

- air polluted by carelessness
- water dirty and undrinkable
- people aiming weapons at each other and destroying cities
- people dying of strange diseases
- some people with lots of money and many with none
- some people with too much to eat and others starving
- many people unhappy and sad and feeling lost or alone.

And for a brief moment, God could not speak. He just watched and watched. When he sat back down, Bubba noticed that a few trickles of tears were coming out of God's eyes, so the angel tore off a piece of cloud and handed it to God to blow his nose. And he did. (It sounded like a rhinoceros, but Bubba was too polite to say so.)

"What happened?" God asked, nearly in a whisper.

"They, uh...they forgot."

"Again?"

"Yes, God. Again." Bubba sat down beside God,

handed him another piece of cloud and winced while the rhinoceros sound bellowed through the air.

All the other spirits and angels and archangels and cherubim and seraphim had vanished, waiting to see what God would do. Only Bubba sat there with God, until there appeared out of a distant cloud a little pussycat face, and then a furry body, and then a long pussycat tail. The cat slowly walked up to God and rubbed up against his leg, then against his other leg, then, with a quick leap, jumped into God's lap and purred while it waited to be petted. Absently, God's delicate hand gently stroked the cat while he talked with the angel.

"How could they forget?"

"They're human, remember? You made them that way."

"Yes, but I thought they would remember the most basic thing about our relationship...that I *love* them and, because of that they can love one another, and the land, and the air and the sea and the animals and all that I gave them to take care of and use for eternity."

Bubba thought for a minute. He knew he was on shaky clouds here, explaining to God about creation, but he was a Texan and Texans take chances, so he went for it.

"They have short memories, God, humans do. And a lot of other stuff gets in the way, kind of takes over their attention, distracts them from what you had in mind..."

"But," God shook his bushy head and squinted up his eyes, "...what can I do to remind them of what our purpose is, of who they are, of who I am, of what the universe is about?"

Bubba crossed his legs, which made his spurs jangle, and rested his Stetson on his knee. The cat jumped from God's great lap and batted at the spinning star in Bubba's spurs. The angel tried to ignore the animal—which he equated with kids and dogs—and looked back at God.

"So are you yankin' my reins or what?" Bubba asked.

"Come again?"

"How come *you're* askin' *me* what to do about this? *You're* God, remember?"

God smiled and showed his one gold tooth in his ancient wide mouth and said, "If I had all this figured out, I wouldn't ask you. Sometimes I need a little help from you..." He pointed down through the hole in the cloud. "...and also from them. You *do* understand the word 'partners' don't you?"

"In Texas we say 'pardners', but, yeah, I get it. You want some help? I'm your man—I mean angel."

"Okay. What do we do?" asked God.

"Send a prophet."

"Done that," God said.

"Send some locusts, or a hurricane, or fahr aints..."

"You mean fire ants..."

"That's what I said, fahr aints, or killer bees..."

"Done that."

"How about a pharaoh, or a dictator, or a hero or

two?"

"Done that."

Bubba scratched his head, then looked at the cat.

"Nobody would believe it," God said.

"Believe what?"

"If I sent the cat."

"How'd you know what I was thinking?"

God smiled again. "There are still *some* things I can do."

Bubba finally said in desperation. "Then good grief, God, why don't you just go yourself?"

"Are you kidding me?" God pulled a thick black book out of a pocket in his saffron robe. "Have you seen my *schedule* for the next million years?"

"Cancel it." Bubba picked up the cat and handed it back to God. "Cancel all of it. This event is more important."

God thought a minute (which on God's watch could have been a century or two) and stroked the purring pussycat. Then he looked back at Bubba. "Good idea. I'll do it. I'll just go down there and appear in front of them all and tell them how much I love them and..."

"Nope. Cain't do that," Bubba said, before he knew what was coming out of his mouth. "Uh...what I meant was..."

"Go ahead. See if you can get the other boot in there and tell me *why* I can't do that?" The cat licked his hand. "I'm *God*, and I can do anything I want to.....can't I?"

"Not exactly," Bubba said cautiously. "Ya see, it's

exactly because you *are* God that you'll scare the bejeebers out of them. They take one good look at you and it'll do 'em in, they won't be able to stand it."

"Stand *what?* I stood under a rain cloud after I jogged and I don't smell any worse than *you* do."

"It's not that," Bubba said. "It's....your *face.*"

God looked at Bubba, not certain how to respond. Then he said: "Now wait just a minute here...what's the *matter* with my face?" He looked at his lap where the sleeping feline was purring. "Doesn't bother the cat."

Bubba rolled his eyes and shook his head. "It's all that *light*, God. Oh sure, we're used to you—but even I have to put on sunglasses sometimes when you get excited about something." He pointed to the hole in the cloud. "And these are human beings. You'd just be too overwhelming for them. They'd be so scared that they wouldn't understand you."

"Then I'll go incognito, in disguise, with dark glasses and a hat and maybe a big moustache and an umbrella and..."

"Not fair. You got to go as yourself, but in a way that they can sort of get to know you, kind of ease on up to you and listen to what you have to say. Like sittin' on the tailgate, sippin' on longnecks."

"Well, how in the world will I ever..?" Suddenly God stood up and the dozing cat fell off his lap right through the cloud and had to crawl back up top using his claws. "I've got it!" God said. "I'll go as a ... BABY!"

"No offense, God," Bubba began, "...but that is one

of the worst, most ridiculous ideas you have ever..."

"NO! It's GREAT! It's a *great* idea!" And God danced around with his hands in the air to music only he could hear, and the cat hid behind Bubba with its eyes staring wide. "Why didn't I think of that before?"

Bubba frowned. "I think you'd be better off as a cat. If you think they're mad about the mosquitoes and flies, wait till the reviews come in on *this* one..."

"And we'll have great pageantry, and a wonderful, passionate story, and a great star in the heavens, and shepherds, and three wise men—no, make that *four*—and animals—some sheep and donkeys and elephants, I love elephants..."

"'Elephants'?" Bubba knew they would have to be deleted.

"...And maybe a barn or something to be born in, and DRAMA, we must have DRAMA, so maybe a small hotel with an innkeeper who..."

"Don't forget angels," Bubba added, almost sarcastically.

"YES!!! ANGELS!!! LOTS of angels!!" God was nearly beside himself with joy at the possibilities. He looked down through the hole in the cloud and pointed. "They'll LOVE it! And they'll *finally* get the message that I love them and they can love one another and take care of each other and the earth."

Bubba pursed his lips. He wondered if he should say what he was thinking.

"How could they do that?" God asked, reading Bubba's mind again. "How could they reject him, this

226

tiny little baby that wouldn't hurt a flea?"

Bubba pointed down again. "They did all *that*, and they keep forgetting. Maybe they don't *want* to hear that you love them."

"It doesn't matter," God said firmly. "We'll keep telling them till they *do* remember. And we'll make this baby story so wonder-full that they'll want to hear it and celebrate it *every year!*"

Bubba shook his head. "I hate to be the practical one around here...but how are you gonna *do* this baby thing?"

God's eyes flashed like a shooting star. "With gusto, with flair, with pageantry—there must be all the important things in the story, like sharing, and giving, and sacrifice, and risk and adventure and, most important of all, love."

"That's not what I meant, God and you *know* it."

"I was avoiding the answer."

"Right—so how you gonna *do* it?"

God motioned Bubba over to the hole in the cloud. They both knelt down and peered over the edge. The pussycat did too and nearly fell over.

"Uuuuuuuhhhhhhh...." God said, looking down to the earth. "I choose *that* one."

Bubba and the cat squinted their eyes. "*Which* one?"

God pointed way, way down to a young couple who were just about to get married.

"She's going to have a baby boy in nine months and it's going to be me—sort of. I mean it will be him *and* me. And our name will be.......uh...let's see, what would I like to be called...hmmmmmmm..." God's smile broadened and the sun gleamed off his gold tooth. "I think I'll be called...JESUS...because in my language that means 'He loves his people.'"

Bubba groaned and sat back down. "Oh no."

"Oh no *what?*" God asked, as puzzled as usual at that anyone could have questions about something which seemed perfectly clear and reasonable to him.

"Do you know how they're gonna try to *explain* all of this?"

God grinned and the wrinkles puckered in his ruddy dark face. "It'll give them fits, I'll bet," he snickered. "But who cares? It doesn't *matter* how they explain it. And it doesn't even matter how I did it. What matters is *that* I did it. I came to them, cancelled my calendar for them, spent time with them and learned from them because I love them and want them to know it, and want them to tell each other the story again and again and again."

"Well," Bubba said, "...*this* should certainly *do* it."

"Great," God said, standing up and stretching. "So get started. You've got a lot to do..."

"ME?" Bubba frowned. "*I've* got a lot to do?"

"Yes, you. I have to go change into Holy Spirit. You go round up some shepherds, and get the star ready, and...oh yes...put some angels on call for the blessed event...scare up some wise men—make one of them a woman, will you?...and it would be nice if there were some music, but I'll understand if Mozart is busy, and reserve the stable in Bethlehem...that nice couple down there's going to need it in a few months—I think it's Mary and Joseph, isn't it?...and get somebody to write all this down in a Bible or something so they'll read the story year after year and remember..." God's voice trailed off as he happily danced through the clouds. "Oh....this will be *so* much fun..."

Bubba hurriedly wrote down a list of all the things God wanted him to do and then flew off all over heaven and earth making the arrangements. Well, the rest is history, Nathan, and we hear about it every year at Christmas, just like God wanted:

"And it came to pass that an angel appeared to Joseph in a dream saying: 'Y'all will have a baby and call him *Jesus.*' And Mary gave birth to Jesus in a stable because there was no room in the inn. And an angel announced the birth to shepherds in their fields who immediately went to the stable to see the baby. And wise men followed a great star which hung over the stable in Bethlehem."

And God was in that Jesus baby, Nate, and slowly got to know us human beings and we got to know him. And Jesus grew up and did things to constantly tell everyone how much God loves them and forgives them and wants the best for them and will be with them in times of change and stability, and gain and loss, and death and life, and pain and happiness. He is there clapping when you hit a home run, and cheering when you catch three fly balls, and listening when you're feeling angry in a time out, and crying with you when you're feeling sad because poor old Rita died.

And just in case you ever forget all that, God has arranged to retell the story of Jesus' birth so you hear it and celebrate it every year at Christmas, for the rest of our lives together, which I hope will be a long, long time.

There are a lot of stories to tell you about Jesus' life, Nathan. I'm sure we'll have some great conversations about them, you and me and Michal and maybe even Bubba. Because that baby Jesus grew up (just as you are) and left his parents and did what he thought best to spread God's message of love and, eventually, to change the world.

I wonder how you'll do that, Nate? Change the world, I mean. In some ways you've already done it, in your Mamma and Papa's life, and in my life, and in the lives of all you touch—as does Rossi and Michal and your friend Sam, and as do we all. Because when God was born into the world in Jesus an amazing thing happened, Nate. At that very same time, God was born into the world through each of us—and is still within us laughing and crying and dancing and running and talking and hoping that we will remember how much he loves us so we can love one another and take care of this earth he gave us.

So this is the end of the Last Letter to Nathan. Like all endings, it is an ending and a beginning, Nate. You're no longer the seven month old baby; now you're launched into life as a young boy. The Christmas letters are over; and we're launched towards new experiences and new stories together.

And if ever the Family Theologian is not around to remind you about the meaning of Christmas, just re-read these letters and remember that baby in the stable who grew up to change the world with love—and let him inspire your own strength and courage to go out and do the same.

I love you very much,

Uncle Chuck

P.S. Bubba said to tell you that God's pussycat was lonely, so when Rita's spirit arrived a few weeks ago she immediately found a place at God's feet, rubbing up against his legs and jumping up in his lap to sleep and purr and be petted alongside the other cat. Bubba says to tell you that God and the pussycats are all doing fine, and that they wish you a very happy Christmas.

ELIJAH

Elijah the Prophet sat in a cave and watched old home videos of Genesis and Exodus and Deuteronomy and ate popcorn and remembered the way we were. Everybody in the known universe (especially the king's wife, Jezebel) was out to kill him for beating up on the priests of Baal, calling down a lightning bolt that reduced the first three pews to ashes, and bringing on a frog stranglin' gully washer to end the drought.

But just when Elijah was having a wonderful wallow in the good old days of the Burning Bush, the Golden Calf, and the Red Sea, there was a knock at the door and it was the Word of God, asking "What are you doing *here*, Elijah?"

"Enjoying myself for a change. Go away. I gave at the office."

Undaunted, the Word of God entices him out onto the top of the mountain where he encounters gale force wind, a Richter 10 earthquake and a blazing inferno. The wind blows through his spirit, cleansing and renewing him; the earthquake makes him move his leaden feet from the routine rigidity of his thoughts; the fire burns through the thick, hard carapace of certainty and the nostalgic notions of maintaining the status quo. Elijah is left sweating, gasping on the ground, surrounded by deafening silence.

Then, deep within him, he slowly becomes aware of a "still, small voice" that gently spreads through his weary, sweating body, reviving and empowering him, strengthening him, reminding him of his purpose, of who he is and what he must be about.

He makes his way back to the cave, where the Word of God is waiting. It says to him "Go. Do something new in my Kingdom. Blow. Unsettle. Burn through the thick carapace of my hardened people that they too may hear the voice recalling them to themselves and to their purpose and to me."

And he does.

And the same is true of us, both as individuals, as a society, as a Church. Changes in our families and in ourselves, changes in our society, new ideas, different values, new and frightening technology, all make us want to join Elijah in that cave with his videos of what is perceived to be the safer past. But the spirit of God comes to us saying; "What *are* you doing *here?*" As we attempt to answer, we are led out of that secure cave to be blown through by the cleansing winds of renewal, shaken loose from our leaden moorings by the breakdown of business as usual, and seared by the fire of the burning needs before us.

Then, and perhaps only then, as we lie exhausted, sweating from our struggle, can we hear the "still small voice" recalling us to our purpose, reminding us of who we are, empowering us to do new things to meet those needs. Then, and perhaps only then, can the Word of God say to us: "Go. Do something new in my Kingdom. Inspire your society, your Church, your work, your family. Take new stands on (temporarily) stable ground, warm everyone around you with your burning to serve."

And that is the difference between faith and nostalgia. Nostalgia calls us back to the cave of what was with the wish it could be so again, perhaps forever. Faith calls us back to the mountaintop to remember who we really are so that we can go forward into the eternal present refreshed, reminded, creatively empowered to serve as we do something new in the Kingdom of God, ready to be asked when we seek shelter once again, "What are you doing *here*, Elijah?"

STRAWBERRIES

Strawberries. When people ask me what was the highlight of my vacation, the wheel of my mind flickers through memories of medieval cathedrals with beautiful stained glass, art museums with Rembrandts and Van Goghs, quaint villages with cobbled streets, wooden shoes and windmills; and when the wheel stops it always lands on...strawberries.

We had just come from a visit to a monastery (Orval Abbey) where the monks make cheese, bread and beer. (The nuns down the road make cookies and jam. I am sure there is bartering.) It had been an expected delight—two stars in the Michelin book, recommended by other people in the hotel, underlined on the tour map. We spent the day wandering the ruins of the old abbey and listening to a monk explain about the newly built one, as we tasted the results of their labor. Our expectations of the Abbey were more than met and we went away with our souls as full as our stomachs.

Having spotted another abbey on the map, which the tourbook said also made the appropriate items plus ceramics, we set out on a quest to find it. The road was long and arduous; we got lost a couple of times and had to make some interesting turns in precarious places; we laughed and used frustrated expletives and told stories about people and places; we ate GORP and drank bottled water as we negotiated the route on the map from the major vena cava down to the spidery veins that would take us to our destination. When I got too close to a ravine (or a truck), or the winding road included obscure one lane bridges, or anything at all looked dangerous, Debi closed her eyes and broke out in hymns—"I was sinking deep in sin..." "On a hill far away..." "Jesus, Jesus, Jesus..."—all of which made matters worse because my own eyes were closed from laughing.

Eventually we saw the abbey in the distance. It seemed worth the trip. The huge twin spires shone in the afternoon sun; the massive buildings sat upon a high mountain overlooking the acres of forest through which we now drove to approach it. But when we parked and went in, there was nothing to see. The inside was stark, devoid of painting, glass or sculpture. The ceramics were done in rubber casts. The beer was harsh and bitter. Worst of all, the bathrooms were broken.

We walked in and walked out. Driving down the hill, we were sorely disappointed that we had spent (wasted) the better part of a day getting there. And to compound matters, our next stop turned out to be a palatial garden where we were hot, uncomfortable, bored, and received the tour in unknown languages (making up our own explanations along the way.)

But on the road from disappointing abbey to the more disappointing gardens, we passed a roadside stand in the middle of nowhere with a hand scrawled sign marked "Fraises." Knowing this meant fruit and not sentence parts, I turned the car around amidst cows, tractors and hymns and, after seeking out the seller in the back of the house, bought a one quart box.

They were incredible. This was the Mother Lode of Strawberries; the Platonic Ideal; the Artist's Conception of What Strawberries Should Be. They were not just red, they were Fire Engine Red, Chinese Red, Madonna Lips Red. They looked like the perfect, shiny, ceramic strawberries that people put in their kitchen bowls to remind them that, somewhere, such things do exist, if only they could one day find them. They were big and sweet and the juice ran down our chins when we ate them, one at a glorious time, sitting right there in the car with the windows rolled down, giggling and slurping and saying "We really shouldn't. But why not? Oh, here, taste this one!" and casting occasional furtive glances back at the stand.

A woman with a car full of kids went past, backed up and carried six boxes into the car. One can only imagine the interior when they got home. She worried us, but there were boxes left. And, immediately after finishing ours, I ran over and bought another one. We slowly, sinfully savoured the entire, wonderful box of strawberries as if we would never see or taste this kind of delight again.

And that is the point. Although we spend a lot of time worrying about the future and trying to know what will happen ahead of time, things are seldom what we expect when we get there. Sometimes they are better and we are happily surprised; the two star Orval Abbey was a four star to me (with five star beer). Often our destinations are nothing like what we expected and we leave disappointed or discouraged. So the destinations, the endpoints, the outcomes, are unknown and unpredictable regardless of how well the tourbook describes them—whether those endpoints are places, or projects, or people's lives, or relationships, or illnesses, or life after death.

But the journey *is* certain; it is known because that's where we are right now, daily, on the way; it is the only thing we have and the only thing we really know. If we focus only on the outcome, look forward only to the destination, we miss the laughter and expletives and story telling and breaking out in hymns or Willie songs. And, God help us, we will miss the strawberries along the way.